TRAGIC MAGIC

WARDS AND WANDS #3

REBECCA ROYCE

Tragic Magic (Wards and Wands 3)

Copyright @ 2019 by Rebecca Royce

Ebook ISBN: 978-1-947672-86-4

Print ISBN: 978-1-947672-87-1

Cover art by Crimson Phoenix Covers

Content Editing: Heather Long

Copy/Proof Editing: Jennifer Jones at Bookends Editing

Formatting: Ripley Proserpina

Published by Rebecca Royce

www.rebeccaroyce.com

Dearest Reader,

Thank you for taking this journey through the Wards and Wands universe with me. This is the third book in the series, the first one being Hexed and Vexed, and the second being Curse Reversed. There is also a novella I wrote with Ripley Proserpina as co-writer for the series called Meow, Baby. I loved writing these books. I loved the touch of realism to the fantasy of this world with witches and humans living side-by-side but not co-existing.

This is the last book in the series, it is time for Ava's best friend Melanie Syed to have her happily ever after. She has been on her own for some time and watched all her closest friends pair off. I am very glad to give her a happy-ever-after, eventually.

I hope you're doing well, and I am forever grateful to you.

Hugs,

RR

For Autumn Reed who I know loves this series. She's an amazing author. You should read her if you're not...

And a special shout out to Becky Stewart for coming up with the title when I faltered a few months back.

As always, Ripley, Phyllis, Heather, Jennifer, Michelle, and Rachel... I can't do this without you.

For Autumn Reed who I know loves this series. She's an amazing author. You should read her if you're not...

And a special shout out to Becky Stewart for coming up with the title when I faltered a few months back.

As always, Ripley, Phyllis, Heather, Jennifer, Michelle, and Rachel... I can't do this without you.

FOREWORD

Dearest Reader,

Thank you for taking this journey through the Wards and Wands universe with me. This is the third book in the series, the first one being Hexed and Vexed, and the second being Curse Reversed. There is also a novella I wrote with Ripley Proserpina as co-writer for the series called Meow, Baby. I loved writing these books. I loved the touch of realism to the fantasy of this world with witches and humans living side-by-side but not co-existing.

This is the last book in the series, it is time for Ava's best friend Melanie Syed to have her happily ever after. She has been on her own for some time and watched all her closest friends pair off. I am very glad to give her a happy-ever-after, eventually.

I hope you're doing well, and I am forever grateful to you.

Hugs,
    RR

*M*elanie sunk to the floor, staring at the message she'd received with disbelief. Maybe if she read it again, it would finally make sense, although she wasn't sure how that could be possible. She skimmed the words once again as though they would change.

Elliot Boothe requests your presence at his home on Tuesday at 3 PM to discuss the legal breakdown of his estate on the event of his death.

She set the paper down. It said what she'd thought it had. Tears she didn't want to shed waterfalled down her cheeks, and she wiped them away. With a flick of her hand, she sent her response. Yes, she would be there. It would be crazy for her not to go. He was a rich, powerful man, and she needed the clients to build up her solo practice or she was never going to make it on her own. Yet... still. Elliot. Dying.

Melanie sucked in her breath. She'd always known he would die early, every member of his family had. It was part of the unspeakable curse, the one that could never be dispelled. It had destroyed the lives of his family for five

1

generations, killed his father, and now was going to take out Elliot. But this was way too early.

His father had been lost in his sixties, a tragedy even then. But this? Elliot was thirty-eight, in his prime, and still, the last time she'd seen him from a distance, a gorgeous man. She wiped her eyes. This was ridiculous. He'd asked her to come do a job and probably only done that as a last sign of respect and honor to her parents, whom he'd loved like family.

Elliot had never really noticed her, nor should he have at ten years her senior. She had been five, drooling over him like he was everything out of a fairytale. He'd barely noticed her then and had been busy with his own life when he was fifteen, as was appropriate.

When he'd been twenty-five, he'd all but ignored her when he visited, and she wasn't sure she'd seen him alone since then. Melanie had been the daughter of his father's butler and head housekeeper. His parents had been generous with hers, giving Melanie access to an elite education she'd otherwise not have had.

She was the witch she was now because of that. Since launching her own law office three years earlier, however, she'd been on the brink of financial ruin. The only thing keeping it open was the fact that she'd always been able to invest money and turn it into profit. But that wasn't going to work forever. She needed the office itself to earn or she was going to have to go back to corporate law, and the idea made her ill.

Working for Elliot would be a great thing, particularly if he recommended her to his friends—before he died a horrible death. Tears flooded her eyes again, but she pushed them away. She stumbled to her feet and wiped at her eyes again. A little magic cleared her face so that she didn't look a mess. It was ridiculous to be this upset over a man she'd not seen in years, particularly since she had always known this end would be coming, even if it was way too soon.

Another message appeared in front of her, and she stared down at it. Melanie could go days and days without anyone contacting her about anything except work and now she was getting two messages in just minutes?

It was an invitation from Ava. She sighed. Her best friend wanted her to join her for a dinner the night after she was scheduled to see Elliot. Melanie loved Ava, they'd been best friends since high school. In fact, Melanie loved all of Ava's people. But lately—for the last three years—she hadn't just been the third wheel in Ava's relationship with her husband and soul mate, Lawson, she'd been the seventh wheel in a three couple group that seemed to get together all the time.

Ava. Lawson. Mitchell, Ava's former fiancé, and his wife and soul mate, Eleanor, plus Stefan and Kim, who had come into the circle with Lawson. Sometimes it was even the ninth person out, when Ava's twin sister Zoey and her husband Elijah joined them. Everyone had always been nice to her, always included her and whomever she was dating into their group. But when she was single—which had been true for the last year since she'd written off men—it had grown far more difficult to see them socially. She was smart enough to know they hadn't isolated her; she'd isolated herself, but it didn't make it any easier to deal sometimes.

What made matters worse, Melanie had become a bad friend, and she knew it. She stared at the invitation. Okay, she'd go. Ava and Mitchell knew of Elliot, or at least that she'd grown up on his estate, and it would be good to see familiar faces after she ventured into the place she'd been avoiding for over a decade.

Too many memories... good and bad assaulted her there. Not to mention her parents had since retired. There was no good reason for her to step foot on Elliot's property.

With a wave of her hand, she called up her daily agenda. There were things to do today. Dressing herself to look the part—a skill she'd learned when she was twelve and she'd scrounged through clearance and second-hand stores so she could look as rich as her classmates—she got ready to go to her office. She had a day ahead of her to do things like obsess over who hadn't paid their bills and try to figure out what Elaine Evans' soon to be ex-husband was doing with all of the money he claimed he didn't have.

Something just wasn't right with what he displayed. He was good at hiding his truths. He'd coated himself in a huge amount of magic, and to others it might look right, but she had always been able to see through glamour better than most.

Her magic couldn't fail her now; her whole future depended on it. Melanie might never find her soul mate, might never join her soul to another person's, but she'd be damned if she lived a mediocre life. She'd promised herself when she sat alone in the back of classes and the mean girls laughed at her for lack of vacation travel plans that no one would ever treat her like she was less than again.

She was almost there.

Melanie was going to make something no one could take from her, something she could be proud of the rest of her days.

* * *

TUESDAY CAME a lot faster than she'd imagined. She'd been up working almost nonstop. The answer to cracking her current case was close. She could feel it in every cell in her body, and her inability to uncover the missing piece of information she needed to win made her want to throw something. But that was neither here nor there at the moment.

Boothe Estate was like something out of a movie. When humans made films about witches—which were usually ridiculously cringe worthy at best—this was the kind of home they put witches in. It was huge, at least three mansions positioned in a triangle around the acreage. She'd lived in the back of the house, farthest from the front driveway. Her family had come and gone as they liked through a back gate few knew existed.

The Boothes had been good to her parents, and kind and helpful to their daughter, but there had never been any question that her family was the help. She'd never been invited to the parties at the main estate or gone on the lavish trips her father sometimes accompanied Elliot's father on.

Mel lifted her hand to knock on the door and stopped. The truth was she'd loved Elliot from a distance with an abandon that could only be attributed to her youth and ridiculous imagination. She'd watched from the lower school as he'd been the king of the upper school, the crème-de-la-crème of the most elite in the witching world.

Living with the curse had made his family what her father used to call "reckless." They earned and lost great fortunes, always knowing they wouldn't have to plan for a full life. They bought expensive items, laughed too loud, screamed louder, and drank too much. They also gave huge amounts to charity and loved each other with an abandon her restrained parents had found disconcerting. She'd thought it was beautiful.

Melanie steeled her shoulders. Enough already. She knocked on the door and waited. As though time threw itself back decades and she was a little girl standing at the door, footsteps approached, making the clicking noise she'd always heard right before someone opened it. Melanie swallowed. It wouldn't be her beloved father opening the mahogany wood entrance to the darkly lit interior, kept that way because the Boothes always hated bright lights as per part of their curse.

The man who opened the door was young. She'd put him around her age, which was funny to think about. Her father had always seemed old to her, but he'd been younger than she was currently when he'd gone to work for the Boothes. It was here that he'd walked into the living room of this house and met her mother.

"Hi." The man's eyes widened, and she understood his reaction. She had almost no ego, but she wasn't disillusioned about her attractiveness. Melanie was physically beautiful and totally disinterested in it. Being gorgeous had never gotten her anywhere except one bad first date after another.

Men who only wanted her for her long legs or big brown eyes were boring with a capital B. The dating scene had never gone well for her.

"Hello." She gave him a bland smile. "I'm Melanie Syed. Mr. Boothe is expecting me."

"Sure." He stepped back. "I'm Edward Jackson. Right this way. Elliot told me that you used to live here?"

They'd discussed it? She rubbed the back of her neck. "When I was a little girl. I grew up here. It's been... almost ten years since I was back."

"Well, welcome home."

Time seemed to have paused inside the house. The smell hit her first. The cleaning products Elliot's mother spelled on the house must still be what the staff now used. Lavender. Chamomile. Mint. There had never been a time she'd scented those things that it hadn't reminded her of the cleaning days. The poor woman had died days after her husband did. Their souls had been truly bound together.

Melanie lifted herself off the ground with a spell. It was habit as much as anything else. If no one walked on the ground, they couldn't make it dirty. The butler had been walking, but lifted off the ground when she did. Maybe it wasn't a rule anymore. Maybe Elliot didn't care if everyone floated or not.

"He's in his office. Right this way."

She knew exactly where it was located but followed him just the same as it was polite. She wasn't a young child learning to fly by dashing through this house when the family wasn't home. She was here to do a job, even if surely Elliot must already possess a team of lawyers who could do this.

The butler opened the door with a magical wave of his hand and closed it again after she was inside. It shut with a click.

The room, bathed in burgundy, felt heavy, like the air weighed more in here. Elliot stood, his back to her, facing the window overlooking the garden outside. He turned his head slightly as Melanie entered the room. She gazed for a long moment, taking in the sheer size of him. He'd grown since she'd last seen him. He was broad shouldered, bulky, like he worked out regularly, though he'd been a skinny teenager. His brown hair had been cut short. Whiskers covered his mature face, but he didn't look old.

He wore dark sunglasses, which told her all she needed to know. The curse really had advanced. Elliot Boothe, the fantasy of her youth, had gone completely blind.

"Melanie Syed." He smiled, not showing any teeth or moving. "You came."

She swallowed. "Of course I did. You... ah... requested my presence." Melanie winced, wishing she could suck the words back in the second she said them. Requested my presence? Internally, she groaned. That was... bad.

He used the desk for guidance as he walked toward her. "Forgive me. I like to stand by the window. I can't see it, but I swear I can feel the light." He touched his sunglasses. "I think

7

with you I can actually take these off. You were here with my father when he passed. You know what the eyes look like."

She nodded before she realized how asinine that was. He couldn't see her, obviously. "I remember what it looked like. You can take them off."

"Great. Because it's like the icing on the cake of this misery that I have to cover up my eyes to not scare little children." He took the glasses off and set them on the desk. He stared at Melanie from across the room, not quite looking at her but in her general direction. His eyes were totally white. Not just the irises. Not the corneas. The entire socket of his eyes were bright white, like the most intense shade of it ever. Neither snow leopards nor the clouds had anything on what the curse did to the Boothe eyes.

Melanie walked toward him, not letting herself overthink it. His father had fallen into a huge pit of depression when this happened to him. She had to imagine that waking up totally blind one day to nothing but whiteness would make anyone feel lonely.

She squeezed his hand, and he frowned immediately before he dropped their linked fingers. His hands hadn't been smooth or manicured but tougher, with calluses that made her wonder what he'd been doing to get them. As far as she knew, he'd never had a profession. He invested money, as his father had before him, and had the Midas touch. Melanie had learned a lot of what she knew from his father, but what could he have been doing that would have given him those hands?

"So…" She needed to say something. "This happened early."

Melanie had always believed the best thing to do was point out the elephant in the room and not pretend it wasn't there.

He nodded. "Seems to be the case. I… I think it's for the

8

best, actually. Get it over with. I was tired of it stalking me anyway. I'd determined very early I would be the last person to ever have this curse. If I couldn't cure it, which I tried to do, believe me, I wasn't going to pass it on. I've been wondering if it's taking me early as a punishment for not procreating."

The way he spoke about it—this curse that had plagued the last five generations of his family—was as though it was a living, breathing thing. Melanie didn't remember his father doing that. But then again he'd lived a full life before it took him down.

"You think the curse... hurried up your punishment... because you didn't find the right woman to have children with?"

He ran a hand through his hair. "I determined very early on that I wouldn't allow this to continue. Even before I saw my father taken down to madness, a shell of the man he'd been before, devoid of magic, shaking in a corner. I wouldn't leave behind any heirs that could take the curse when I died. It ends with me."

Melanie swallowed. She remembered as the bright, happy young man he'd been when she'd secretly followed him around. He'd decided even then that he'd be staying alone his whole life? Not have any children? There was a tragedy to that, to accepting his solitary state, because circumstances that were never his fault took him down.

There really wasn't much to say. She had to keep it together. Save for her early fantasies, she didn't really know him, and expressing huge emotion would hardly seem appropriate. "I don't suppose you've tried any new practitioners who do this for a living? Who could take the curse off your family?"

"Every possible one. No, this is ending and that is why I'm so glad you could come." He motioned toward the desk.

"Don't mind me. I'm going to try to smoothly walk to my chair and sit down like I am perfectly capable of making my way blindly. I'm not flying because that goes even worse than walking. And… my magic is already depleted enough. I can't seem to spell myself places so I am fumbling around forever, unable to see."

It wasn't that he was in the dark either. Melanie remembered enough of his father's ramblings toward the end. It was like being stuck in a perpetual bright light that never let you see anything because of its luminosity. Eventually, in addition to the curse taking his magic, this would drive him insane. Sleep was virtually impossible.

He made it to his desk, only banging his leg once as far as she could tell. It was impressive that he could find his way at all. Her father used to help Mr. Boothe get around, but Elliot was still doing things himself. Maybe it was just early days.

She took a seat in the chair across from him. "How can I help?"

It took him a moment to answer, as he tried to orient himself. Or at least that was what she imagined he was doing. "It's hard for me to picture you here, Melanie. The last time I saw you… you were very young, I think."

He'd seen her once as a teenager but paid her no attention. That didn't surprise her at all that he didn't remember even if what was left of her teenage heart wished it was otherwise. "I don't think we interacted when last I was here. I was a teenager. You were older." She cleared her throat. "I think the last time we spoke I was quite young. I was surprised to get your note."

"It's been a long time since I interacted with someone that I didn't know what they looked like before I lost my sight. You are a first for me. I'm trying to imagine the person with the voice." He tilted his head. "I don't suppose it matters. I locked myself up in this house to wait out the end in privacy.

My staff has directions to not let me out when I start raving later on in the progression. I'm giving myself the gift of not being remembered publicly for what this will to do to me." He paused and took a breath. "Forgive me, I'm rambling."

She loved the sound of his voice, could have listened to it all day. "Well, I am… tall, I suppose. Almost six feet. And my hair is very dark brown." Or at least it was when she left her natural color alone. She'd been many different shades over the years. "Like my father's. I look like my mother, otherwise. That's what they tell me."

He smiled. "I have a sense from that, thanks. It helps that I actually know your parents. Are they well? I spoke with your father, and he told me what you were doing. That's what gave me the idea. He seemed fine. Is he?"

It was sweet that Elliot was even thinking of him given the current state of things. "He is well. Sustained some damage to their home in the weird tsunami a few years ago, but that seems to have been worked out and fixed, finally. There was a whole ordeal with getting the city to pay for it."

The time had been miserable for Melanie. She'd kept Ava's secret that her father caused the tsunami while trying to get her parents through the bureaucracy of the witching world to get their place fixed. It would have been so easy to turn around and sue the Blakelys for what happened except Melanie only knew in confidence, and she'd never do that.

In the end, it had worked out, but the hours spent feeling like she'd betrayed one person she loved for another had been what finally made her go out on her own, leaving her corporate job. Life was too short to be unhappy every day.

"I'm glad to hear that. I don't think I knew they'd been affected." He winced. "But I wasn't great at paying attention to small things I should have been attentive to. My father wouldn't have liked to have known I didn't take care of that."

Oh, she hadn't meant to make him feel guilty. "Please

don't worry. Your family was so generous with mine. They were well taken care of in so many ways. They have everything because of their years with your family. All is well. How can I help you?" She repeated the question.

This was hard. So much harder than she thought it was going to be, and she'd imagined it would be tough. Seeing him brought down like this and being back here... she was well on her way to feeling like she would always be not quite good enough in a world of stuck up witching families.

How was he still so gorgeous even in the midst of this? That was a whole other issue. Obviously, she'd never really gotten over her fascination with Elliot Boothe.

"You're a solo practitioner. That's almost unheard of in these days of conglomerates. I need someone like you. When your father told me what you were doing, I got the idea to hire you to help me set these things in order before I pass on and they're all left for viewing in public records."

Now, he spoke a language she could understand. This was what she did. "I never cared for the big corporations. What things do you need set in order?"

"Hundreds of years of records dating back to before my family was cursed. I need to make this all orderly, filed, or destroyed—what legally can be—and I need my estate set up to go to various charities and people. I need all of this done fast. I'm rapidly fading. I don't know if we have months. Melanie, I need you to help me get this ready before I am lost to the madness."

CHAPTER 2

The same feeling of helpless distress struck Melanie hard as she listened to Elliot. This time, however, since she was alone and she had some semblance of decorum and how to behave with a client—which Elliot Boothe was about to become—she managed to keep from sinking to the floor. She kept her face stoic, not that he could see it, but the act of trying alone made her keep her emotions in check, and her voice the correct amount of sympathetic and yet professional.

"So soon, Elliot? Do you think it's going to go that fast?"

He nodded. "It's racing through me. My father's slow decline is not present here. Maybe the curse is angry because I didn't procreate and pass it on. I don't know how all this works. I always said I'd be the last to go through it, and so help me I will see to it that I am. But maybe there's some rule long forgotten that says it makes it worse on the person deciding that. My father was so convinced he'd beat it, as was my grandfather before him, that neither considered not living an ordinary life. The men in my family and their utter

13

egotism." He shook his head. "Will you help me? Let me hire you?"

She needed the money. Her own investments were only going to keep her tiny company afloat for a little bit longer. Not to mention… this was Elliot Boothe. The man of her dreams to whom she'd silently compared every boyfriend and first date and found all of them lacking.

"Sure." She nodded. She'd done it again. She had to remember that all answers needed to be verbalized. He couldn't see what she did.

His smile was huge. "That is so… great. You can't imagine how stressful I found the idea of having strangers going through my family's things. Again the ego, this time mine, kept me from doing this years ago. I thought I'd have more time."

She chewed on her lip. "I have a pretty big case going on right now. I can't talk about it, obviously, but I'll tell you what I can do. I'll take care of everything in relation to that one in the mornings and come here in the afternoons. Unless that doesn't work for you. Not that you have to be here for me to go through the paperwork and start making up the estate documents." She just sort of hoped he would be.

Elliot shook his head. "I have no plans." He pointed to his eyes. "This is all I'm doing between now and death."

Now, that was truly tragic. "There's nothing you still want to do?"

"The things I spent my time on required sight. Well, all my senses, really. I'm not going to do any of them half-assed, if you'll excuse the language." He waved his hand and a contract floated down toward her. "It's a non-disclosure agreement. Obviously, you'll want to read it. You're the attorney, but it's the same one I've set out for everyone dealing with me in this time in my life. It basically says you can't talk about what's happening to me until after I'm dead.

Then, if you want to go on the television and talk about it, feel free. I'll be dead. I won't care, presumably. Right now we still have holdings and investments, and any discussion about my decline will plummet stock prices in the few things we still own. That will negatively impact the charities and people I want to set up. Otherwise, I actually don't give a shit what people think of me anymore."

She took the paper into her hand. "I'll read it tonight and let you know if I need to make any changes."

"Great. Then can I expect you tomorrow?"

She'd done this enough and been raised as the child of the servants to know when she was being dismissed. "Absolutely. See you then."

"Well you will, I'll hear you and speak to you but not actually see you." He grinned, and she winced. Yep, bad choice of words, that was for sure. Even if he made a joke out of it. The point was taken. He would never see her again.

In fact, she didn't know how old she'd been the last time he had. It was possible Elliot had never viewed her as an adult, had no idea what she looked like. The idea threw her even though it really shouldn't matter. She was probably a memory of a child to him in terms of how he visualized her, if he did at all.

She pushed the thought about. He'd talked about his ego, and it turned out she had one as well. Melanie might have liked him to think she was pretty. Smart, professional, good at her job, talented, and kind... all of those things, for sure. But yes, pretty. Oh well, he was cursed. She wasn't going to make this about her.

"I'll... be in your presence tomorrow, then." There, that should be better. She sincerely hoped.

He nodded. "It was a stupid joke. Cursed humor. You'll have to excuse it. I've got to laugh or I'll just... be angry and drunk all the time. Even that would be too pathetic for me. Big plans tonight?"

Well, that was an abrupt shift she had to roll with. He wanted to know if she had plans? "I'm seeing friends tonight, actually. Dinner party or sorts. There are probably going to be two former and one current Enforcer there. One of whom has removed a curse that I know of and probably hundreds that I don't. You don't want me to ask them if they'll try?"

He ran a hand through his dark hair. "Sure. Feel free. I've had countless Enforcers here trying that. Bring your friends if you think there's a chance. They won't find anything, but it's worth a go. Tell you what, as we tear down all but the walls of my estate in preparation for the end, you have my permission to have anyone you want try to remove this. I won't have it said I didn't give it the old witching school try to survive and recover. Enjoy your party. I took those times for granted. Friends. Normalcy. Until tomorrow, then."

And just like that she was somehow employed by Elliot Boothe in his quest to set things in order before his untimely death. Life had a way of taking sharp left turns she never saw coming.

* * *

AVA AND LAWSON'S house had evolved over the course of their marriage. Lawson lived on the edge of the best part of town but never crossed into it. That was very different from Melanie who had taken the first chance she'd gotten to move to the right neighborhood and inserted herself into society that way.

Not that they ever accepted her. They didn't. But she could afford to be there—or at least she had been able to when she'd been working for the big firms—and that was where she'd been determined to be. But in Ava's house, they didn't seem to be concerned with any of that. Ava had been born into the right society, one of the richest families in town, and Lawson was the head Enforcer. They didn't worry anymore about the things that still plagued Melanie. Maybe it came from finding a soul mate. It certainly did seem to make people... content... in a way she'd never been.

Or maybe she was just all worked up because she'd seen Elliot and it brought her whole childhood to the forefront of her mind again.

She knocked and entered after the come in. Ava had a tremendous amount of power now but hadn't for most of her life. They still did things the human way around her from habit if nothing else.

Melanie was a few minutes late and so it wasn't surprising that the room was filled already with people. It was the usual crowd. Ava and Lawson, Stefan and Kim, Eleanor and Mitchell. They were a strange grouping considering Mitchell had once been hexed to leave Ava at the altar. But in the end, it had all worked out. Melanie looked around but didn't see Zoey or Elijah there. "Well, hello there, everyone." Melanie put on her best version of a happy smile. "You all look wonderful."

Everyone turned to welcome her and soon hugs were exchanged and greetings made. There was a motion to doing these things, like hugging and hellos were a wave that moved from one part of the room to the next.

It finally ended with Ava who pulled her close. "Are you okay? You're almost never late."

"I've had quite a day, actually. I can't talk about it. Client privilege." Even as she spoke, she realized that wasn't entirely true. She could discuss this with some of the people in this room. Elliot had said she could bring in Enforcers. She'd do that, after she got them to sign non-disclosure agreements. If they would do that. The Enforcers were pretty much permanently on a non-disclosure agreement.

"Work." Ava nodded. "Come in. Let's get seated. We actually have news this week."

Melanie smiled. They always had news. It was part of what was so interesting about these dinners with Ava. Her best friend winked at Melanie. "We're pregnant. Decided, finally, to just do it."

The tears that flooded Melanie's eyes surprised her. "Oh, Ava," she managed to choke out. "That is the most beautiful news, ever. Congratulations."

Ava stopped, holding her tightly. "Melanie... I... Thank you."

She managed to suck in her tears. What a way to make an entrance. Apparently, she was going to be on the edge of hysterics all the time now. But it was a beautiful thing. Babies. Weddings. After seeing Elliot so brought down... it was lovely to know that life went on in positive ways.

It was a joyful dinner, everyone talking over each other, and laughing. Ava would be the first of Melanie's close friends to have a baby. Ava's sister, Zoey, didn't count. Outside of being close to Ava, Zoey and Mel had never been close. Melanie didn't know Eleanor well enough to ask her about her future plans to have children or not have them. The two had grown closer over the years but still it was one of those very private conversations that she was never going to initiate. If Eleanor wanted to talk about it, that was one thing. Asking was an invasion of privacy.

And as for Kim and Stefan? The ex-Enforcers, with ex seeming to come and go as they saw fit, had never struck her as the settle down and have a baby type. But really, what did Melanie know?

What made someone want kids and someone else not want them? It was a very personal decision. These were the kinds of things she thought about when she watched everyone laughing and congratulating her best friend on the upcoming beautiful addition to their family.

"Melanie, I heard about you today." Lawson set down his drink, and she turned toward him.

She arched her eyebrow in reply. "Really? Should I be worried?"

"Maybe." He nodded and that was concerning. "I wouldn't share this except that I trust everyone in this room. Are you somehow involved with Peter and Elaine Evans?"

She'd half-expected him to ask her about Elliot. The Cursed family was famous but maybe not a huge concern to the Enforcers. Instead, he brought up the divorce situation she found herself in. "I'm sorry, Lawson. As you know, I can't confirm or deny clients. So while that might seem like I'm saying yes by saying that, what I'm really saying is that you know better than to ask me that since I'm not going to answer."

Was there anything more awkward than telling someone no in their own house? She rubbed the back of her neck. Give her a courtroom to argue in any day of the week and she was fine. Telling Lawson no at his dining room table? That was harder.

"I could make you tell me. Enforcer to citizen."

Ava groaned. "Lawson."

"You could," Melanie had to agree. He wasn't lying. He absolutely could stick her under investigation and ask her anything he wanted. "I still wouldn't tell you. Then you'd lock me up. And have to get a magistrate to give you permission to force me magically to speak. You wouldn't get that which would leave you with no choice but to illegally do so, which would mean you'd have to wipe my mind afterward." She'd thought about this at length. "That's such an imprecise thing to do. Most of the people who have that happen end up spending their lives in healing hospitals. And I think that would upset your wife." She winked, hoping to lighten the mood. Maybe they could talk about the new Bomber play getting ready to start at the local theater.

Stefan threw his head back and laughed. "She's got you there, boss."

Lawson leaned forward. "I'm actually worried about you. Peter Evans is not to be trifled with. He's scary and so far untouchable. We've had him on five different extortion and misuse of magic cases. He always gets away with it. As this woman is his fifth wife and every large firm in town refused to represent her and given that your name is now popping up on radars that he's asking about you, I'm going to assume that you took her on."

She waved her hand in the air. "Are we talking in circles? I think I answered this."

"Just be careful. This is a man who destroys our most sacred traditions. He convinces women to marry him for reasons other than being soul mates and then divorces them. Can you imagine having your soul connected to a person and then having it ripped away? The fact that he has done this over four times…"

Melanie knew the circumstances of this better than Lawson did. She'd spent countless hours with his current wife-slash-victim-slash-she-kind-of-did-this-to-herself person. Yes, he somehow managed to do what few witches would ever consider: to soul bind himself to person after person—like it was a game and not an older than time binding ritual that so few people wanted to get out of that the law was fluid and difficult to manage on the subject.

Lawson shook his head. "You're not listening to me."

"No," she sipped her drink. "But the good news is that I appreciate that you are doing this out of concern and not because you're trying to be meddlesome."

"Okay, enough." Ava sighed loudly. "You made yourself understood, my love." She kissed her husband's cheek. "But Melanie is a big girl, and if she is somehow involved in this, I'm sure she's being careful. Because she would never not be." Ava glared at her as she spoke those last words.

Her husband was clearly not done. "I may have you followed."

That was enough. She pointed at Lawson. "Where do you get off thinking that you can..."

He interrupted. "You're family. That's where I get off."

Melanie sighed and made a split decision. Mitchell and Eleanor had done work for the Enforcers a lot lately. He was a historian who could track incredibly difficult historical information and Eleanor had developed quite the reputation for being great at figuring out curses. As far as she was concerned, they'd all count.

"I'm changing the subject." A non-disclosure agreement appeared in front of all of them as she let her magic do the talking. "I do need help for another client. He's one I imagine most of you know. And I have his permission to do this. If you sign those."

Stefan and Kim both grabbed theirs and after reading it signed it. Mitchell laughed, but he and Eleanor did the same. Lawson opened and closed his mouth several times before Ava signed hers without looking toward him. It was a lot to ask for people who dealt in secrecy to be told their word wasn't good enough. Melanie understood that. But she was doing it because she was skirting the line of what she was ethically comfortable with anyway.

Lawson finally affixed his signature with his magical wave. They'd all signed.

"I'm doing some work for Elliot Boothe. You've signed a NDA so you know that means you can't tell anyone."

"Wow." Kim grinned at Melanie. "You are having a very exciting time right now."

"Catch me up." Eleanor looked between them. "Who is Elliot Boothe?"

Her husband took her hand and kissed it. "The Cursed Family."

"Oh." Her eyes lit up. "Sorry. I only knew that description. I feel terrible. I was the crazy girl for a while. I get how awful the names are."

Melanie leaned forward. "I grew up on their estate. My parents worked for them as their house staff. I watched the curse take down Elliot's father and now, a lot earlier than expected, it has gotten him. I have his permission to speak to whomever I like about trying to get him some help—if such a thing is possible—but the truth is he's setting his affairs in order and doesn't want the family's holdings to plummet with this news. He's basically in hiding."

Kim winced. "I'll go see him tomorrow. I never have. I'm not sure I can do what a million super strong curse removers haven't been able to do, but I can try."

"And I'll make him something," Ava offered. "A special drink concoction that might make him feel better. If you can get me something of his I can get working on it. I need something from the person."

That was sweet of her. Mitchell sat forward. "I'd love to track the history of this. I never have. I…"

Eleanor put her hand on his arm. "I'm still not as fluent in this as the rest of you. Back up, please."

He smiled at her. "We all went to the same school as Elliot Boothe. We have a little bit of a… fascination with him. Such a troubled, difficult family, and yet he was the golden boy. When we were young there was no one more popular or beloved."

She couldn't have put that better herself. Ava met her

gaze. Yes, her best friend had known what no one else in here would. Melanie'd had it bad for him when she was young and it had never really let up. Ava might not know that last part, but her intuitive friend was catching on now. Maybe the Earth was even speaking to her, which was really weird to think about.

"His family is cursed?"

"Father to son," Stefan answered for the group. "For generations now. Mostly curses, as you well know, Eleanor, having survived a heck of one yourself, are located on a person. But somehow the Booths have been cursed in such a way that when one dies, the next son in line gets the curse thrust onto him. I don't remember all the details of what happens, but it's nasty."

In that Melanie, could help fill in what she needed to know. "Starts out feeling like a flu. They're not sure if they're sick or not. You can imagine how terrifying that would be. Then, it all goes downhill from there. Blindness but not just oh, can't see. Their eyes become pure white, like spiderwebs of white cover them. They lose their magic bit by bit after that. Eventually, they lose their minds. And then they die in terrible pain with no idea who or what they are."

She took a sip of her drink. The room had gone quiet. It was one thing to ooh and ahh over the Cursed Family story but the truth was it was a tragedy. "They are also incredibly rich. Generation after generation. They can turn one dollar into one hundred with no problem. They're generous. Kind. They were good to my parents—and to me. I'm with all of you because Elliot's father sent me to school and saw to it that I got in. He paid for it. His son seems to have taken the same path. The difference being that he's deliberately fathered no children. It stops with him. I'm going to help him get his affairs in order. But maybe we can save him? Or you people can. Between the six of you, you've gotten a curse off

Ava, rid the world of serial hexers, found and destroyed an ancient witch who had cursed Eleanor, and if I'm not mistaken, had something to do with that serial killer who turned the Addingtons into cats." That had been a strange affair, the details of which were kept sketchy. "Maybe you can save him. I haven't ever done anything like that, but I do have you all as my friends. Maybe I can help by just knowing you."

Ava's smile was gentle. "We'll see what we can do. I promise."

That was the most she could ask. Instead, she pointed at Lawson. "Don't have me followed. That's creepy and intrusive."

"You just defined Enforcers." Kim grinned. "Creepy and Intrusive. It's pretty much what they do."

Everyone laughed, including Melanie, although she wasn't particularly jovial. "They? You're officially not an Enforcer anymore?"

"Nope." Kim touched her stomach. "Ava isn't the only one with that announcement."

Ava pointed at her. "You have no idea how hard it is has been to not say that to you. I knew I heard him or her in there last week."

That was incredible. And it answered the "did they want babies" question. Melanie supposed that was the end of it. Kim couldn't be an Enforcer, at least not when she was pregnant. She got to her feet and hugged the other woman. As she did, she lifted her eyes to Eleanor.

The dark haired beauty shook her head fast. "No, don't look at me. Not until I'm done with school. And I want to get a PhD so a few more years at least."

Mitchell tugged on the end of Eleanor's hair and they shared a moment. Lawson had said earlier how strange, how awful it was, that Peter Evans kept sharing his soul and taking it back. How heart wrenching it must be to do so. Melanie would never know that herself, not unless things changed for her, and they certainly didn't seem to be moving in that direction. Witches were careful, they chose wisely, they bound themselves for eternity, and when they did, it seemed like they needed the other's presence more than they did food or water. The other half of their soul was as essential as breathing.

Ava and Mitchell had almost made a terrible mistake. It was obvious, and of course hindsight was twenty-twenty, but they were both so better off with who they ended up finding. The universe was careful in witch pairings. What did it mean that Peter kept doing this? And how awful was it that Elliot Boothe, with all that charisma and joy in his youth, had decided to never seek it, to never share his soul? To leave the world without any touch of him still here, not connected to anyone's soul?

Melanie stepped away from the table. No wonder her first dates went so badly. She was nothing but sour and difficult, even in her own head.

CHAPTER 3

*M*elanie stared at the woman in front of her and tried not to hate her. It was a bad idea to hate clients. She couldn't remember actually hating anyone she'd represented before. Elaine Evans was the first. Mel sipped her coffee and listened to Elaine talk. Part of the problem, and this really wasn't Elaine's fault, was that the sound of her voice was maybe the most annoying sound Melanie had ever heard. She really wished she could be the kind of person for whom those things didn't matter, but she'd never tolerated other people's small annoyances very well. Maybe it came from living on her own as long as she had.

She just did better by herself. But then again, she hated being alone, so it was a constant battle between her heart and her… problematic personality.

Melanie might have been overthinking this. Maybe Elaine was annoying, end of story. It wasn't like she didn't know that Peter Evans had married and left wives before. She was his fifth, and every time this happened, it ended up being reported upon all over the witching world. Those wives all left the country and refused to be questioned. Elaine had to know what she was getting herself into. That didn't mean that she didn't deserve good legal representation just because she was some kind of idiot. The trouble was Melanie couldn't get her to tell her why she'd done this, and it was the missing piece of this whole mess. Well, that and several bank accounts containing a lot of money that Elaine believed she was entitled to at least half.

Considering how she lifted the end of her sentences like she was asking a question even when she wasn't, it was hard to know when she needed to answer and when she didn't. Mel was about to ask the woman to talk more.

"I'm sorry to interrupt you." The woman had been going on about something unfair that was happening to her in the separation. Melanie really didn't care. "But we have to talk about the things we're not talking about. I've had a searcher spell out for some time now for those missing accounts. As he's done this before, your husband has hidden those accounts pretty securely. It's my magic versus whomever he hired to do it. I'm good, but as I've told you before: I don't have the resources to battle the hidden magic all the time." Melanie drummed her fingers on the desk. "Having more information would be tremendously helpful to me. It's like I'm battling your husband's immense resources with one hand tied behind my back. Please let me help you. Elaine, you can trust me. I promise you can."

The woman's lip trembled. "Sometimes I can't believe what an idiot I am."

"We're all idiots sometimes." Melanie could come up with a dozen things she'd done in her life that had been utterly stupid. She'd made so many missteps she couldn't even count them anymore. At no point did she ever imagine she'd be her age, alone, and still trying to make her business work.

Elaine rubbed her eyes. "I... I can't talk to you about what you want."

It was that word—can't—that caught Melanie's attention. Sometimes it was what people didn't say that you had to pay attention to and sometimes it was about the details. She leaned forward. "Elaine, are you unable to tell me? Because you've been magically spelled not to?"

The other woman wept, not nodding, not indicating in any way that it was an affirmative answer to Mel's question. That was response enough. To even have given that much of a yes had to have been painful as hell against a magical spell placed on her. That kind of magic was criminally illegal.

For the most part, witches used magic like humans used technology—to make their lives easier. Melanie didn't know any witches who owned a ladder. Not since Ava finally came into her powers. Why bother ever having one? They could float up and around wherever they wanted. Humans invented things to make it possible for them to do with science and tech what witches did naturally.

But there were limits, and they were self-imposed most of the time. When they crossed a line of acceptability, laws were made. Curses, hexes, spells of ill-will, they were all banned and would place the practitioner in the arms of the Enforcers. A silencing spell fell into that category.

How long had this woman been suffering like this? Melanie chewed on her lip. In her job, she saw the worst of the world, never the best, and yet still the low depths that people would ascend to never ceased to surprise her.

"I'm going to get you some help."

Elaine's lip trembled. "Be careful. He'll go after you."

"I'm not worried." She really wasn't. Magical bullies didn't scare her. Not anymore.

* * *

SOMEWHAT MORE SUBDUED than she'd been the day before

thanks to her morning, she made her way to the Boothe estate. Edward opened the door for her, noticeably checking her out in a way that made a muscle in Melanie's jaw tick. She didn't think he meant any harm. He was just looking, but to do it so obviously just showed a lack of subtlety that bordered on pathetic. Internally, she sighed. "Hello, nice to see you again. Is Mr. Boothe here?"

He nodded. "Mr. Boothe is always here. Back to the study, that's where you'll find him. That's where he spends all his days." He cleared his throat, and Melanie knew what was about to come before he said it. "I was wondering if I could take you to dinner sometime."

That was sweet. But boy, he did not want to date her. She'd been at this long enough now to tell the ones that were going to go badly and the ones that were going to be worse. Those men practically came with flashing lights that said: do not attempt an evening with this one. Dater beware. He was a man who couldn't hide that he was looking at her ass. He was too unfiltered for Melanie. She lived in a world where women got cursed into not being able to speak their truths. Where it was possible for the Elaines of the world to physically be unable to speak about what happened to them. What would she do with Edward and his earnest expression?

"You don't want to date me. I'm a mess." She smiled at him. "Trust me. I come with so much baggage you'd need to float ten of them in here just to bring all of my stuff. But I have a girlfriend, Jaiden, you would love her. She's pretty much the complete package, and I think she would love you. The handsome, strong, caretaking type is just what she loves. What do you say? Six feet, blonde haired, blue eyed. Your type?" Melanie had always been good at this. If she got a feeling she should set people up, they inevitably ended up married. That might even have been a magical thing for Melanie. She'd never pursued it. "She just moved back from Hoangtown. Never had time to really date before."

A million emotions crossed over Edward's face before it ended in a bright smile. She ignored the pang that came from knowing she'd caused him momentary pain and embarrassment. It was hard to ask people out, tough to take that kind of risk, and miserable to be rejected. But she'd spared him the pain of dating her. That was what it would have been for him. She was sure of it.

"I'd really like that." He scratched the back of his neck. "Can I get her contact information?"

"You sure can." She waved her hand, and Jaiden's information floated over to him. "She's free tonight."

"Ah..." He laughed. "Well, this went differently."

Melanie couldn't set up everyone who asked her out, but this one would work. She was sure about it.

She turned and quickly made her way to the study. Elliot leaned in the doorway and floated backward when she entered.

"Working on the floating. That was nice of you, what you just did."

Melanie blinked. Even the sound of his voice could send her into butterfly flutters in her brain. "Ah... what?"

"Finding him a date. That was nice of you to do that. Do you set up everyone you reject?" He stopped floating when he hit the desk behind him. She winced. It was hard to fly blind but even walking would be a problem if he didn't know the room completely.

She sat down on the floor and then placed her bag on a chair in the corner. "Not every person who asks me out gets set up with a girlfriend. Sometimes I get a sense, and I do it. It's just a flutter in my mind. I hardly notice it, and then it turns out they are meant to be together. Can't really explain it."

He laughed. "In ancient times you'd have been the most important woman in town, the paid professional matchmaker. People would have traveled for months on end to introduce you to their kids."

"What a completely horrifying idea." She shuddered. "No thanks. How are you feeling today?"

He sank into the chair behind him. "Still figuring out how to get myself around without colliding with furniture. By the time I've mastered it, I'll go crazy and be restrained in bed anyway."

"Oh, I'm sure we can figure out how to get you used to the proximity of things before then." Surely, there must be services to help. Even if they went to the humans.

"Melanie..." Elliot grinned. "I was making a dark, obviously bad joke. I don't need your help with this. At least not yet. I collide with things sometimes but mostly I'm fine. It comes with the territory unfortunately."

She scratched her head. "Maybe I don't have much of a sense of humor."

"Maybe I make you nervous and sort of uncomfortable because of my white eyes and blindness. Plus the whole cursed thing. I bet you laugh plenty when you're elsewhere." He sighed.

She had to correct him. "I tend to be a pretty serious person."

"Well then, someone has to spend his life—or her life—figuring out how to tempt your sense of humor to come play."

How had this conversation taken place? It was... bizarre. "Um, well, not so far. His, by the way. I do prefer men in that regard. Although I think I would have accidentally eaten Edward for breakfast. I'm not easy. It's tough to date me, and I wouldn't wish the task on anyone I legitimately like, so

31

there is the problem laid out nice but not neatly. I see you've brought boxes in."

Elliot leaned back on the chair. "Well, technically I had Edward do it, but yes. I think this is all of them. There might be more of them in the garage. I'm going to ask Edward to look there tomorrow. But for now, I think we won't even get through this today, so it's good enough to start with."

She smiled. "We are barely going to make a dent unless this goes remarkably faster than I think it will. All right, so here's what we're going to do…" Melanie took off her blazer and set it aside. He couldn't see her, but she was still dressed professionally, even wearing pantyhose under her black skirt. Her white blouse was buttoned all the way up.

Melanie took a seat in one of the chairs by the desk. "I'm going to make three piles. One for things we're going to keep for one reason or another. One we're going to discard. And one we're uncertain about. Then afterward I'll divide the keep into separate piles. And figure out the maybes. I'll read them to you, and you can tell me what I'm looking at if I can't sort it out. Sound good?"

He nodded slightly, barely a tilt of his chin. "You'll probably know better than me. This is legal, obviously, but it's also posterity stuff. My family saved everything. There might be some things people want to see. The Cursed family. It drew enough attention during our lifetimes."

That made sense in a sick, twisted sort of way. It was like they were a circus attraction and had been drafted for life in the big top tent with no consent of their own.

She snapped her fingers. The papers in the first box would travel over to her and then went where she directed them using her magic. It was a minor spell, barely registering on the Richter scale of her magical ability. The box was his paternal grandfather's, and it was evident right away that the man had saved everything. As a lawyer, she appreciated the diligence. There didn't seem to be a receipt he'd thrown out during the year they went through.

Elliot stayed attentive to her questions about every slip of paper, every note she went over for about three hours, and then it had just been too much for him. He placed his head in his hands. Mel stopped talking and watched him for a second, not exactly sure what to do. It was interesting to spend this much time with him. In the past, when she'd fantasized about him, she hadn't known how good he smelled. That was the first thought that struck her. It was a combination of the freshness of a woodsy soap and sandalwood, her favorite combination. That really shouldn't surprise her. Everything about Elliot had always been her favorite everything.

He was also tapping his foot on and off. It was like he had a steady rhythm in his head. It wasn't an obnoxious sound, easily tuned out. Yet, she actually found it kind of soothing, in a weird way. Should she say something about his having hit a wall?

She bit her lip. His father used to get exhausted simply trying to get through the day. "Hey, would it be okay if we took a break?" She rose. "I could really use some food. Want to go get some with me? Off the clock? Two people who need to eat."

He smiled, lifting his head. "And she lets me off the hook for falling apart for a second. Sorry, sometimes it hits me hard. Yes, you should go eat. I don't leave the house, so I won't be joining you, but thank you for the offer."

His father had quit leaving the house, too. But he'd had a wife and a son who visited. Plus, her father and mother had been around, a lot of people to speak to. Elliot was alone with Edward who didn't seem to hover too much or really be looking out for him as far as Melanie could tell. Maybe that was preference from Elliot. Still, it had to get lonely.

"Well, I'm not really in the mood to go out. I went to a dinner party last night. Speaking of which, you should be hearing from my Enforcer group. They want to see if they can help you. They all signed NDAs..."

He cleared his throat. "I trust you to handle that. I'm beyond being able to manage that kind of thing myself."

"Right, well, how about if we bring food in? I could use the company without having to get restaurant ready."

He nodded once. "I'd like that. I don't remember the last time I ate a full meal. I mostly just make do with whatever scraps I put together in the kitchen after Edward leaves for the night. Last night it might have been cheddar cheese and pickles. As I'm not pregnant and having weird cravings, that didn't really do it for me."

No, that didn't sound appealing at all. "How about if I bring in Italian?"

He rubbed his stomach. "I could really go for some Italian."

So could she.

* * *

AFTER SHE'D ORDERED the food by sending her magic to the restaurant, she got busy setting up the kitchen for them to eat at the table. The few meals she'd taken at the main house when she'd been a child she'd eaten in the kitchen. The family ate in the dining room, but tonight Elliot would have to adjust and eat with her where the staff used to be. She doubted he'd care, and it was a weird, leftover feeling of not wanting to be somewhere she didn't belong when she stepped into the dining room.

Maybe people didn't really ever get over the lectures they got as children. Stay out of the dining room, Mel. That's for the family.

A popping sound filled the room before Kim appeared before Melanie. She smiled, taking off her sunglasses. "Sorry, I'm so late. Long day. Don't ask. I will be glad to be officially done with Enforcer things someday."

Mel lifted an eyebrow. "Someday? Do you think that'll ever be? I can't see you and Stefan ever stopping. Not even when the little one comes."

Kim patted Melanie on the arm. "I'll be lucky if he doesn't wrap me in the proverbial bubble wrap and keep me locked up somewhere with the baby to never emerge. In the meantime, I get to keep working until he finds a way to encourage me to stop. Stefan always manages to get his way with me eventually. I never could resist him."

Melanie had gone to high school with Stefan. She hardly remembered him. In school, she'd had her sights on one thing and that had been working her way up and out so that someday she could belong. Stefan had been on the wrong side of the tracks and seemed like he held everyone on the so-called right side in disdain. She couldn't remember having one conversation with him before he'd popped up in Ava's social circle several years ago.

To Melanie, maybe the best part of Stefan was his wife. Kim was somehow both kind and scary. Melanie wasn't even sure how she pulled that off.

"Let me tell him you're here." Melanie stepped away from Kim. "He doesn't see a lot of people or go anywhere anymore."

Kim nodded. "I'll wait here. I read up on this today. I think the chances that I can help are…"

"Slim to none." Elliot floated toward them. "Hi, I'm Elliot. I can't see you, but if you're here, I'm going to presume you're one of Melanie's Enforcers."

Kim winced, but he'd not had to witness it. She straightened after a beat then walked to him. "That curse is all over you."

He nodded. "You can see it so you're better than half of the people who try. But just because you can see it doesn't mean you can remove it. Am I right?"

Kim placed her hand on his arm, and Melanie liked her even more than she had a minute ago. It was amazing how many people wouldn't go near the Boothes. As though the curse was contagious. It was lunacy. That wasn't how these things worked, but Mel had seen it over and over. Elliot's father hadn't shut out the world and some of those who had come in had done so with utter horror on their faces. Even without sight, Melanie had to believe there was a feeling a person might get when they were in the presence of someone who found being around them nightmarish.

"You're right. I can see it but that doesn't mean I can fix it." She closed her eyes and then opened them. "It's the fastest moving curse I've ever seen. I can't get a grip on it. Like it's..."

"Fluid," he answered for her. Clearly, Elliot had heard this before. "Thanks for coming and looking. It's just one of those things. Unfortunately, my burden to bear. I do appreciate you taking the time. We were just about to have dinner. We can order more. Are you hungry?"

Kim rapidly blinked. "No, thank you. That's very nice."

Melanie couldn't imagine that too many people offered Enforcers something to eat. Most of the time they were probably just ousted from the house.

Elliot turned the force of his white gaze to Melanie, and it moved through her like a hot gust of air. She rubbed the back of her neck. He took a breath and squared his shoulders. "How about you, Mel? What can I get you to drink? We have so much wine in this house that will have to be distributed to someone after I'm dead. Do you want to help me drink some of it before I can't anymore?"

Kim looked between them, lifting an eyebrow. Melanie wasn't sure what that was about, but it quickly passed.

Elliot smiled. "I'm getting you the wine. End of story. It was my father's passion. The Boothe men all fixate on something. Used to take me to this place in France. An old town. It should be thriving by now with the wine enthusiast boom, but it never did. It's practically abandoned. Doesn't make sense really. Why some places thrive and others don't."

Melanie had seen all sorts of receipts for that place. A small town in France. Elliot's grandfather had spent a lot of time there, too. "I will take some wine."

Kim shook her head. "I'm pregnant so I'll have to decline and..."

A pop sounded again and this time a drink floated in front of Melanie. It was a smoothie. Mel smiled. She was used to this from Ava. The woman was always getting readings from the Earth that her friends needed certain nutrients and then sending them on to them with no warning.

"Someone else here?" A muscle ticked in Elliot's jaw. Despite his relaxed appearance, he was obviously tense.

Melanie touched his arm. "No, but it seems you have been sent a drink from my friend Ava. She's an Earth healer, and she gets... signals as best as I can understand it... that people need certain things. I put you on her radar. You're going to get drinks."

He put out his hand and snapped his fingers. The drink came to him. "Thank her for me. If I get the chance to meet her, I'll thank her myself."

"Will do." Melanie turned just as the food arrived onto the table.

Kim stepped back. "I'm going to think about your issue,

Mr. Boothe, I'm not just running away and saying oh well, done. I figure out how to fix things. It's what I'm good at." She hugged Melanie briefly. "See you soon. Have a good dinner."

"Thanks," Melanie answered as she tried to read into whatever Kim wasn't saying. There was something in her tone and it was Mel's job to figure these things out, usually. Still, she didn't have time for Enforcer maneuverings. Not with the current workload she'd taken on.

Plus, she'd never admit it, but she was very glad to have Kim leave as she popped away. It wasn't right that she felt that way, but Melanie wasn't above admitting to herself she liked to have Elliot's attention to herself. She'd had it all day and there was something addictive about it. Elliot could focus, even with his white eyes, better than anyone she'd known. One word from him was worth ten of anyone else.

She walked to the table and sat down. Okay, she had to pull herself together. This was rapidly getting out of hand. He was a very nice, cursed, dying man. If he could see her, there was no guarantee he'd like what he saw. She was pretty, but beauty was always in the eye of the beholder. Melanie had to keep her head on straight. That was all there was to it.

CHAPTER 4

*D*inner with Elliot turned out to be fun. Melanie couldn't remember the last time she'd enjoyed eating with anyone as much as she did with him. It helped that the food was so delicious. Warm, tasty pasta and chicken coated in cheese meant she was going to have to do twice as much exercise when she got up the next day, but she loved every second of it.

Elliot sipped his wine. "I was the first Boothe not to grow wine."

She stared at his hand as he held the stem of the glass. "Why didn't you?"

He smiled. "I had other interests." He set down the glass using his hands and not his magic. It was the first thing she'd seen him move unmagically the whole evening. Everything else had been spelled into working. "I can't remember the last time food tasted this good."

His answer had been cryptic, and the lawyer in her wanted to pry. *Your honor, I ask you to magically compel the witness to answer the question.* But she was enjoying this too much. Melanie could always read witnesses, what they said and what they didn't. It wasn't different with Elliot. He knew he hadn't answered, and since she'd officially known him for about five minutes, she was going to leave him be on it.

"Surely, even if you don't want to leave the house, you could order the finest food in the world delivered here." That was one of the gifts of their lives. Magic made everything easier. Humans had to use phones. All witches had to do was spell something into happening. They could have gotten the food straight from Italy if they'd wanted to. Local had just seemed simpler since she knew the menu. But he didn't need to eat whatever he found in the fridge.

He tilted his head to the side. "That's true. You're one hundred percent right. It's very easy when you're in this condition to forget that you still can do things. I don't know if that's the nature of the curse or just because of what happens with the vision, but it starts to become much more normal to do nothing, to speak to no one. The fading away from life... it happens slowly, but it happens." He smiled, which took some of the edge off how sad what he said to her was. "Tonight has been a nice reminder of what it is to have dinner with a beautiful woman."

Her cheeks heated, which she was glad he couldn't see. "You don't know I'm beautiful."

"Oh you are. I heard Edward's reaction to you and what you said about your baggage. You're beautiful. Dangerously so."

She set down her own book. "It has never done a thing for me, what I look like. I'd rather people know me for other things. Although, I think about it. I'm a living, breathing person. I do have some vanity."

"Honesty." He nodded once. "An admirable quality. You don't pull punches. Living and breathing. Yes, that you are. As opposed to being... dead. Like a ghost."

His mind jumped from one topic to another in the most interesting ways. "Ghosts?"

"Sure, ghosts. Everyone claims to have seen a ghost here on the Boothe estate. Even Edward and he's almost never here after dark. Didn't you? In all your years living here? Your parents did."

Had they? They'd never mentioned it to her. "I must not be creative enough to be visited by ghosts. They don't come say hi to me. No, I've never seen them and my parents never mentioned they had."

His smile was huge. "They didn't want to scare you. There are five ghosts that usually hang around here. The main on the third floor. My great-great, oh who can remember how many greats, grandmother who periodically appears in the music room. That was the one I think that your mom used to see regularly. The gardener still tending the roses out back. One no one knows the identity of in the attic and then the most recent one is a jilted lover of my great-grandfather. She sometimes shows up in my bedroom. I can't see her anymore, but I can hear her creaking the floorboards."

Melanie drummed her fingers on the table. "A walking witch ghost. Do they lose their ability to fly when they are dead?"

He threw his head back in laughter. "I'll have to ask her."

"Please do, I'm fascinated." She realized what she'd done when he stopped laughing abruptly. This was the problem she made on dates. They'd been having a lightweight conversation about ghosts. He'd been teasing her. And she'd just turned it uncomfortable. Did they lose their power to fly when they died? What was the matter with her? This was always when the dates—not that this was a date—went askew. They either decided she was someone they wanted to sleep with and be done with or simply be done with her altogether.

She was just too much. Why couldn't she keep things light?

That was why his grin staggered her into silence. "Fascinated. Well, then I most certainly will ask the ghost when next she presents herself to me. I haven't heard from her in a while but then again maybe I'm just not aware that she's there because I can't see her."

"You're serious about this."

His smile was almost cat-like. "Completely."

"I guess I can't be too skeptical about ghosts. An ancient witch, who had somehow managed to keep her energy around for hundreds of years, possessed a friend of mine temporarily. She wanted to use her body to take over the world. It was a big ordeal a few years back."

Elliot raised his eyebrows. "How did they fix it?"

"I'm not sure. That is where the story goes vague because the Enforcers got involved. I'm not sure how the outcome got to the happy ending they have now, just that it did. And she devotes her life to studying ancient things."

He reached forward like he was going to grab something and then winced. A second later he waved his hand and the dishes rose from the table and headed for the sink. "I was going to be gallant and do that with my own two hands. I guess I forgot for just a second I couldn't see and that I've made no moves to become any kind of functioning blind person."

That was true. There were lots of blind witches and they weren't banging into things. His father had been better at maneuvering around. "Why don't you? Take some time to get better at it?"

"What would be the point?" That was the first time Melanie had ever heard him sound bitter. Not that she could blame him. She'd have been wracked in much more anger and resentment than Elliot seemed to be if this was happening to her.

She reached across the table and took his hand before she squeezed it. His face softened as he squeezed back. "I think you might be the first person to touch me in... I don't know how long... who wasn't trying to fix me or check on my curse. You just... touched me. For no other reason than the moment itself."

Now that made her officially tear up. With her free hand, she wiped it away. "I... I'm not sure what to say to that." And she was so rarely at a loss for words.

He let go of her hand and sat back in his seat. The amused expression he tended to wear—that she now saw for the cover it was—returned to his face. "What are you doing tomorrow night?"

She steadied herself and put back on her own cover, which was the detached sound of her voice. They could both do this act, pretending they didn't care what he was going through. It certainly did make things easier, although totally false at the same time. "I'm going to see the new Bomber play."

Elliot sat forward. Well, that had certainly gotten his attention. "Really? You like Bomber?"

She cleared her throat. "I do. I mean, who doesn't? If you take away the mystery of no one knowing who the elusive playwright is, the plays are still brilliantly touching. Oh, and when he does a musical? Just as good. I'd love to know who he is. Or she. It could be a woman. And some people are speculating that it's actually a group of writers. Like all writing under the name of Bomber."

His smile was huge, and she had no idea what that was about, but she'd certainly made him happy and that was something, at the very least. "Really? Is that what people say? Yes, I like Bomber, too."

"Well then you should go. I'm sure we can get you a ticket."

He waved his hand in the air. "I'm good. But tell me what you think. I mean, tomorrow is Saturday, right? I hope I'm not losing track of days."

He was right. She worked on Saturdays, most weekends, but that didn't mean she should come by here. That was inappropriate. Lest she forget, and she almost had, this was her client. Wow. She had to pull it together.

"Tomorrow is Saturday. So we can talk Monday about it." She got to her feet. "And I should get going."

"Oh." His smile fell. "Well, tell me Monday what you think of the show. And by the way, do you have any idea how those Enforcers do that pop in and out of places that they do? I'm powerful, always have been, but I don't have the slightest idea how to do that."

She shook her head. Getting out of the habit of non-verbal communication was harder than it seemed. "No, I'm afraid that's a trade secret for them." Although she'd seen Mitchell do it, and he wasn't an Enforcer so it was clearly something that could be worked out. "I'm afraid I'm not that powerful. I always scored mid-to high level but not gifted on the power scale. I wouldn't even attempt it. Even if I could figure out how to move myself in that way from this room I'd probably end up face down in a sewer."

He snorted before he outright laughed. "I wouldn't know where I'd ended up. That would be a disaster. Still… something to contemplate. I never gave it much thought before. But it's that sound… the pop. It makes me jump. Shows up a second before they do. Weird, right?"

"It is." She stepped away. "Goodnight, Elliot. Do you need me to lock up or clean up anything for you since Edward has left?"

He waved his hand. "No, I can do that. Goodnight,

Melanie. Be safe getting home. I wish I could go with you to make sure you got home. It's late, right?"

A little after ten, which wasn't so late for her to be out. "I'll be fine."

But it was ridiculously sweet he'd thought of it, and she rode that ridiculous high all the way home to her own apartment.

* * *

It was a dull Saturday as she once again found herself searching for the money Peter Evans was hiding. She yawned. In some way, she had to figure out how to have a life beyond work that didn't include fantasizing about Elliot Boothe. Her nighttime dreams had been... hot to say the least. His strong arms drawing her down from where she'd been on top of him. They'd both been naked, her breasts aching, but no penetration, not yet...

She blinked. That wasn't helpful. Particularly because in her dreams he'd had his bright blue eyes as he stared at her, not the white of the curse. She sighed. Fantasy had no use in her life, never had. Maybe it was time to use a matchmaking service and just deal with whomever she got matched with as a life partner. How bad could it be? As long as it wasn't Peter Evans it couldn't be much worse than this.

Mel leaned back in her oversized chair and stared at her beige walls. She'd never do that. Being alone wasn't so bad. Witches who settled for anything less than the real thing found themselves being Elaine Evans. A message floated in from Jaiden, her friend she had set up with Edward. The date had been a dream. They were going out again tonight. She smiled. Yep, she was good at that. Maybe she should make her own matchmaking service.

In another life, when she was gloriously rich and able to

open any small business she wanted on a whim. Woo, what a life that would be. She supposed she could actually make that happen. She'd invest what little she had left, and then when it was big enough, she'd buy a storefront. She closed her eyes. No one was going to take matchmaking from an unmatched witch. Besides, her temperament was entirely wrong for the job. Hearing people whine about their love lives and why they weren't working might just make her go completely nuts. It was hard enough to hear her personal inner dialogue.

Melanie rose. It had been a boring day, but it was almost time for the Bomber show. She wasn't going to be late or miss it. Staunchly staying away from reading reviews, she had no idea how the show was being perceived. But it was only the fifth night since it had debuted, so not everyone who'd wanted to see it would have gotten to do so yet. That was what was so strange about the Bomber shows. They were always very limited in engagement, and this was the shortest yet. Three weeks and then never again.

The theater made its money back and the actors got paid, but the author could do a lot better if he/she/they ran a longer showing. Maybe it was all part of the mystique of the whole thing. Rumor had it this was the last one. That the author wouldn't be writing anymore. If that was true, then it really was a tragedy.

A ping caught her attention, and she went back to the documents appearing on her desk. Had something substantial turned up? She read the document, her smile broadening with every word she read. Yes, this was the break she'd been waiting for. They had to get the magical inability to speak about Peter's business off of Elaine. They needed answers. But Melanie had just found his hidden cache of funds, at least one of them, and it was a heady amount of cash. She'd done this all on her own. One of the things her power had always allowed her to do was chase answers.

She was glad to see that hadn't changed. On Monday, when Stefan and Kim came by to work on Elaine, they'd get even further down this path.

Things were really starting to look up.

* * *

THE SHOW WAS BEAUTIFUL. She sat next to Ava and wiped away silent tears as Ava quietly did the same. At first, she'd been struck by how different this play was from all the others she'd seen by Bomber. In the past, even when they were musicals, the shows had been about bigger than life issues as told through the lives of ordinary people.

This one was told on a much smaller scale. It was a father and son tale. They'd never understood each other, and they had little time to get to the point of understanding since the son was dying. His life was cut short through a disease magic couldn't cure. They'd never come to understanding with each other about his mother's death, which may or may not have been caused by a negligent act of the father.

Elliot had been right to not go see this. He didn't need this emotional pain coupled with everything else he was going through. She pushed the thought aside. Her obsession with him had to be gotten under control. She forced herself to be back in the moment.

She was the seventh wheel tonight, and she didn't even mind. This was too beautiful to spoil. Looking around, she could tell she wasn't alone in feeling the moment. Lawson, Ava, Mitchell, Eleanor, Kim and Stefan were equally as enthralled. This was real pain... and in the end, everyone felt it the same way.

This play was beautiful. It would haunt her forever, but she'd be glad she'd seen it.

* * *

"WHAT DID YOU THINK?" Eleanor swung around in the parking lot to ask Melanie. "I mean, I loved it. I'm so sad, but I adored it."

"Me, too." She smiled at the other woman. "I just…"

"Melanie Syed," a male voice called out, and she swung around to see a man charging toward her whom she'd never seen before. He raised his arm and a jolt of magic struck Melanie backward before it abruptly stopped.

The man shouted, but as Melanie collapsed on the ground, she could hardly think. There was so much pain…

"Stefan," Kim shouted. "I've got her."

The world went black and that was such a relief.

* * *

SHE WOKE up to the sounds of incantations. It was the healer's chant. She'd heard it, unfortunately, quite a few times through illness and injury in her life. Three faces stared down at her. She didn't know any of them, but they all wore the white healer robes she recognized immediately.

"Wh-what happened?" She had to clear her throat to get through the words. "Am I okay?"

The blonde woman on the right placed a steadying hand on her arm. "You're lucky they got you here so fast and that Kim was there to work on you at the scene."

The whole event rushed back to her. "I was attacked."

The idea seemed foreign, like it had happened to someone else and not her. She sat up and the chanting stopped. "That's right. Take it easy. You've been unconscious for three days. You're lucky it was only that long. You had a kill shot from a magical assassin. If he'd been able to get the whole dose into you, then you'd be dead. The Enforcers were on scene to stop him."

Lawson. Stefan. Kim. Yes, the man had only hit her for a second. What a terrible, awful way to die...

She'd only had a touch of it. Her tears surprised her, and before she could rein them back in, she outright wept on the shoulder of the blonde healer who didn't seem surprised nor bothered that Melanie was so abruptly losing it. Someone had tried to kill her. She could have died, and she'd hardly yet lived.

If Mel vanished from the world today, her friends would miss her for a while and her parents would mourn her, but it would eventually be like she'd never existed at all. That was not how she wanted to be... this was just...

"Melly?" Her mother's voice caught her attention, and she was soon transferred from the arms of the healer to her mother's comforting embrace. "We've been so worried about you. The healers said you would be fine but still... you're okay. You're awake. All right, I can breathe again."

"You can, but I'm sure you're smothering her," Mel's father spoke from behind her mom.

It was okay. She was a grown woman with responsibilities, and she knew how to take care of herself. But she'd never been so happy to have her mother hold her as she was in that moment.

A thought that should have come earlier clouded her brain and made her try to speak through the sobs. "Who did this? Why?"

"I can answer that." Lawson strode into the room. He wore his serious Enforcer expression but lost it for a second when he saw her. She really must look a mess. "You okay, Mel? We're all so worried about you."

She wiped her eyes. "Obviously, I'm not."

"That's normal. It's a result of the attack. The magic that pushed into you upset your whole system. Victims usually report that they feel off for several weeks before regaining their equilibrium. You'll be okay. I'll have Ava make you something; it will help. She's wanting to do something. I sent her home a few hours ago to rest. She's hardly left. Eleanor, too. They love you."

That was sweet but beside the point. "Lawson? Who? Why? What?"

"Peter Evans. I guess you've made some headway he doesn't like."

The account she'd found. "I know where his money is. Someone has to get to Elaine."

"I'm afraid she's dead; he took her out first. He must have someone on the payroll who protected his soul from the affront." He squeezed her hand. "And I'm sure that account is gone. It's most likely been moved. We'll get information from the assassin and have him locked away where he won't be found until trial. We're looking for Evans, but he's vanished. Not for long, I can find anyone."

She choked on her sob. Oh poor Elaine. That woman had been so… broken. Witches didn't do well when their other half, the person who held the other half of their soul, died. Elaine's death would have hurt him soul deep if he hadn't made arrangements. Melanie wasn't even sure how this worked.

"We have to get you somewhere safe."

A safe house? She was going to have to go to an Enforcer safe house? They were places even bad guys couldn't find. Her mother shuddered. These were the places of legends. Sometimes they were said to be dungeons or underground. Melanie sobbed again. She just couldn't seem to stop.

"I'm sorry." Lawson bent over. "I promise it won't be so bad."

It would be somewhere where she wouldn't see or speak

to anyone until Lawson had this under control. Maybe, considering her current situation, that was for the best. She nodded. "Okay, let's go."

She didn't have to be assaulted again to know she was in over her head. Still, for just a minute it had felt good to think she was the one who was going to get Peter Evans. Now she might never know why the man did what he did... and poor Elaine. She was very annoying, but she most certainly didn't deserve to die.

Before this, Melanie would have thought herself brave, would have believed she could handle anything that came her way. She even joked with her friends that they didn't call on her when they were cursed or hexed when she could have helped. She knew better now. Melanie, in her heart of hearts, was a coward. She had to stay away from these kinds of things. As soon as it was safe she'd return to the corporate world. It was soul sucking but safe. She wasn't cut out for this. Not at all.

And if part of her knew that her thinking wasn't rational... well, she just didn't care.

For two days in the safe house, she slept on and off. The place was magically spelled so food was replaced whenever it was used, and she wanted for nothing except company. Even that she didn't miss much, not at first. What her body needed was sleep and the drinks that popped in made by Ava. They did make her feel stronger.

But on day three, loneliness set in. She had television to watch, mostly of the human variety, and books galore, but the being totally alone bit was going to be a problem. Lawson had promised to come back every several days as long as it was safe for him to do so.

She thought about Elliot constantly. He was dying from a curse he'd known was coming for him, that would take his mind, and yet he was brave about it. She'd had one moment and fallen apart. She wiped her eyes. Stupid tears. She was sick of them, too.

Did he notice she hadn't shown up? Who would he ask about it? Or would he just write her off as disinterested and not remember her for more than a second?

"Stupid, Melanie. You're his lawyer. Not his girlfriend. Not even his friend. He's probably annoyed he has to hire someone else. Pull your shit together. Use this time to... I don't know... be a better person."

Somehow she had to.

CHAPTER 5

The pop woke her a second before Lawson appeared by her bedside. She screeched, pulling her blanket up before the room lit up with light.

"Fuck, Lawson. You terrified me." Her heart raced, and she had to physically calm it down. This would have terrified her when she wasn't half out of her mind.

"Sorry, I wasn't expecting you to be asleep. You were the last time I came, too, and you didn't wake up. Are you okay? Still feeling sick?"

Melanie loved Ava, but she wasn't sure she could understand how Ava loved and lived with a person who so completely misunderstood the basics of emotions sometimes. "I'm... not okay. Did you need something? Also, what else am I supposed to be doing? It's not like there are a lot of distractions around here. Sleeping seems the thing to do."

He ran a hand through his hair. "I know, and I hate keeping you like you're a prisoner. We've come up with a solution. Well... a solution was presented to us. Do you want to get dressed?"

She looked down at herself. Yes, talking to Lawson not dressed was just weird. "Give me a second."

"Sure, I'll be in the living room." He popped away. That sound was starting to grate on her. Pop. Pop. Pop. Did they have to do that all the time or could they sometimes just float around or—gasp—walk like the rest of them? Maybe she was just grumpy.

Melanie whirled her magic around her, changing into clothes, and walked, deliberately, into the living room. "Sorry. I wasn't expecting guests."

He sighed. "Ava says that when you're feeling vulnerable you go for surly. I'm going to assume that little sarcasm is that."

"Go ahead, assume that." She tilted her head to the side. "What's up?"

"Elliot Boothe reached out to us. Several times."

She swallowed. He had? "Well, he's my client that I'm currently working with and a friend of my parents." She'd leave out her other feelings. If Ava had told him about them, there was no point in adding to them, and if she hadn't, Mel would spare herself this conversation.

Lawson and she had once threatened to transmorph each other in school while they were arguing. Things were not always calm between them even if they now felt like family.

"Right. Apparently when you didn't show up for several days, he reached out to your mother who filled him in. I wish she hadn't for safety reasons, but what's done is done." He held up his hand. "Don't get mad. I've spoken, gently, to your mother. She won't share again. Elliot got in touch with me and let me know that Boothe manor is as safe a place as there ever was. I disagreed until I checked it out. He's right. The place is a fortress. He doesn't have all the safety precautions on, but when he does, you really can't get in there. Even me. I had to work like a dog to get through. It would certainly be enough time to get to you. And we can place an anti-tracker spell on you that means you can be there instead of in one of our anti-tracker houses. A little unusual but… everyone hates the thought of you being locked up indefinitely."

Melanie swallowed. She knew exactly what he meant by making the place a fortress. There were spells on it that kept people from getting within a mile of the gate, which was only possible because they owned the land for miles around it. If Lawson thought the spells were strong enough…

She wiped her eyes. "I'm like a faucet. Yes, I'd like to be back to civilization. But I don't want to put Elliot out. I'm sure he's doing this as some sort of favor to my parents who he loves."

Lawson made a noise she couldn't quite decode and then suddenly took her with him in a rush of magic where she landed on her feet in the middle of the Boothe house. She jolted. "A little warning, please."

"If you're not used to it, it does no good to brace yourself." He stepped back. "Better to just get it done, like ripping off a Band-Aid."

"That's a human thing," Elliot spoke from the doorway where he leaned against it. His eyes were covered in sunglasses. "I'm sure Melanie spell casts her bandages on and off. She doesn't rip the skin away."

Lawson grinned. "True. I spend so much time with humans, sometimes I sound like them. I'm going to go. We think you'll be safe here. If that changes, we'll move you again. Don't worry, Melanie. Peter Evans is going down. Criminals like him have no place in this world."

Just like that, Lawson popped away, leaving her in the living room with Elliot, in the middle of the night. She wiped her eyes. He couldn't see them but it made her feel better. "He's gone. You can take the glasses off if you want."

He pulled them from his face. "The Enforcers are coming

and going so I've been wearing them. I've gotten good at feeling their arrival. Even before the pop there's a ripple in the air. Hard to explain. Might be my other senses finally strengthening a bit."

"I… I can't express enough how grateful I am to you for doing this. I know your privacy is important to you and…"

He moved swiftly through the air until he was in front of her. "Stop. This is nothing. You're… okay. That's what's important. I'm so cut off here I hadn't heard what happened, and it wasn't until I reached your mother and she told me that I found out you'd been so badly hurt." He cupped the side of her face. "Mel, this is your childhood home. I can't think of anywhere better for you to heal. Besides, you'll be doing me a favor. Edward is in love, and his head is in the clouds. That's thanks to you. It'll be nice to have company that can stay focused on a conversation."

She laughed, the first time she'd felt like doing that since the attack. "It's safe here, but you're placing yourself at risk."

"I'm already at risk. I'm cursed, remember?"

"Elliot, I'm not myself right now. I don't know how long it's going to be until I can get back to work. You might want to find someone else to help you. I'm a bit of a mess. I keep crying. Lawson says it's a natural response to the kind of magic I got hit with and it will stop, but I don't know when and…"

He hugged her. It was such a strange sensation to be in his arms. Maybe it shouldn't have been, he was touching her face just a second before, but this was more intimate. She closed her eyes and pressed her head against his shoulder. When she realized what she'd done, she tried to pull back, but he held her steady. "You're going to be okay. I promise."

"I work for you. I… you don't have to… that is to say… this is inappropriate and…"

He sighed. "Let's take a break with the 'you work for me'

part. For now, let's call this a pause. You can go back to working for me soon but not for a while. Deal?"

She laughed. "I'm not sure that's how it works."

"Sure it does. We're pausing the working for me thing. We'll just be here. Okay?"

She was so relieved to not be wherever it was that Lawson had put her. It felt like she could breathe in this house. There was someone else to talk to. "If you don't mind having a person in your house who is alternating between crying and sleeping all the time for however long it takes for the residual magic to leave my system."

"That's fine. We'll just take it easy."

Elliot waved his hand, and it sounded for a second like the house groaned. She jolted, but he held onto her. "It's just the security magic turning on. I haven't used it since my father died. But it'll be like a fortress now, impenetrable. I promise. That man isn't getting anywhere near you, but we can let people in that you want to see. Lawson also put consensual spells on Edward, your mother, your father, anyone who knows you're here, so it makes it impossible for them to discuss it. That way it can't be accidentally spoken about."

All right. It was time for her to put her big girl panties on and pull it together. So many people were working to help her when the truth was she'd done this to herself, taking a case she knew was dangerous and dismissing Lawson when he'd brought it up the first time.

"Thank you. I... I should go lie down in the servant's house. I can..."

He shook his head. "Unless you have some strong need to go back there and stay in the exact room you slept in as a child, stay here with me. As safe as I just made us, I'd really rather have you close." He winced. "Not that I can do anything particularly useful to protect you. The whole I can't see thing. But still, it would be nicer to have you here. I don't mind company if you don't."

She wiped her eyes. "I don't. I'll go make us some food."

"I should offer, but I was never good at that even when I could see." He spoke the words, but he didn't let her go. "In a second, okay? I've been a little... worked up, thinking you were out there unprotected and someone had nearly killed you. I know we barely know each other, and technically, you were working for me, but I think of you as my friend."

She smiled. Friend wouldn't have been what she wanted years ago when she dreamed about being with him. Where they were now, however, in the way that things had turned out, friend seemed pretty damned wonderful. She'd just put aside the fact that sometimes she still dreamed about him now.

"Say something. I just said a pretty ridiculous thing, and I'm out here dangling with it." She loved the laughter in his voice.

Melanie pulled back to look at him. "I had a huge crush on you when I was younger. Like for years and years. Never in my wildest imaginings could I have thought we'd end up hiding out in your house and really becoming friends. Thank you for being you." She stepped back. "There, now I said something ridiculous, too. We're both hanging out there."

He widened his white eyes. "Wait. What? Really? You're kidding."

"No." She flung her dark hair over her shoulder and headed for the kitchen. "For years. I'd hide under the table and watch you. Sorry, guess I was an early stalker."

He followed after her. "I really had no idea."

"Why would you? Most teenagers aren't aware of the fascination a five year old has with them. It would have been weird for you to notice. Do you like chicken?"

He nodded. "I do. I mean, I like all food. Thank you."

This really might be okay. She stared out the window as she headed to cook them something to eat. All she needed was for the scary stuff out there to stay away until Lawson could arrest Peter Evans. Then life could return to normal —with some major changes she'd be making to see to it that she learned this lesson. She wasn't invincible, and acting like she was cynical and didn't care wasn't working for her.

She was soft inside.

* * *

"Do you like music?" Elliot asked her all of a sudden as they were finishing dinner. She was having a hard time staying upright in her chair and maybe she'd missed the transition to it somehow.

There was a flush to his cheeks, an alertness to his manner that was different than he seemed most days when they were working on the estate. She tilted her head to the side and stifled a yawn. "I really do. All kinds. Do you?"

He nodded. "I love music. It's what I do most nights. That and watch movies I've already seen. I can see them in my head since I already know what they look like. I was thinking about going into the living room and listening to some for a while. Do you want to come?"

"Oh, I don't want to get in your way. You should do what you were planning. I'll clean up and…"

He reached across the table and found her hand. It took him a second, but he did manage to do it without knocking anything over. "Mel, I'd love the company. I didn't used to be so completely solitary. And since you don't seem to mind my eyes or want to run away scared, I'd really love to have you listen with me. It's a new artist, purely strings."

Melanie yawned. "I'd love it, but I don't think I can keep

my eyes open. I'm not usually a sleeper. Like maybe four hours a night max, but I keep having to go to bed."

He nodded. "Don't worry. Another night. And I won't let it get loud so it bothers you."

This was his house. He could play his music as loud as he wanted. "I really don't want to be a bother..."

He held up his hand. "Stop. You're not. Take any room, Mel. Even mine if you want it. I don't sleep anymore, not really. Maybe an hour or two every few nights."

That wasn't good news. The constant bright light could make the person crazy, and it had to be hard to sleep. If she recalled correctly, he'd quickly move from no longer sleeping to losing memory and forgetting things he'd always known. Then the madness set in and it was over after that. She swallowed down the sob that threatened. This had been hard to think about when she didn't know Elliot at all. Now getting glimpses of what a good person he was would only make this harder. Added to the fact that she was already a mess? Yes, a retreat to her bedroom was what was called for.

"I won't take your bedroom. What an idea." Melanie tried to laugh. "Thanks. I'll go find one of the open ones and settle down for the night. Maybe tomorrow my energy will come back."

He touched the side of her face, rubbing his thumb over her cheek. "I made you sad when I told you that I wasn't sleeping. Hard for me to tell things like that right now because I can't see, but I could tell, almost like I could feel it. I'm sorry. You actually know what that means. It helps for me to be able to say it."

"The Curse has always been this burden you guys bear. I hate it for you. And you don't need to worry about how what you say or what you're going through affects me. That's for me to deal with. You can live your truth, Elliot."

He nodded. "Get some sleep, Mel." His smile broadened.

"Besides, tomorrow you can tell me all the things that you liked about me during your so-called crush phase years ago. All of them."

She groaned. "I'm already regretting telling you about that."

"Can't take it back now. I know."

She smiled all the way to the bedroom she picked out. It had been easy choice for her. When she used to play in the house, the room with the butterfly wallpaper had been her favorite. The house was old and no one had bothered to update the decorations in the rooms they hardly used. As there hadn't been a female born in the family in at least three generations, this room was thought to have been Elliot's great-great-great-great-aunt's room. She'd died in childhood and the room had remained cleaned but relatively untouched ever since.

Melanie had loved it as a little girl. The room had always seemed inviting, like someone should live in it, play there, surrounded by the butterflies on the wall. She touched the wall now. There was no dust anywhere. The cleaning crew did a great job of keeping the place looking like it wasn't closed off and unused most of the time.

She lay down on top of the bed, barely managing to kick off her shoes before sleep washed over her.

The house was quiet, and she just couldn't force her body to stay awake any longer.

Unlike the nights in Lawson's safe house, she dreamed. She was alone, heading from her office to her car. Looking down, she could see she wore her hated black high heels. They pinched her feet but looked fantastic with her black suit that she wore to court. It was a funny detail to focus on. She hurried, there was somewhere she was supposed to be.

"Melanie Syed," the voice called out to her as it had done that night after the show. She whirled around and this time as the magic hit her, she went down to the ground, pain overtaking her until she couldn't think at all.

A gentle hand touched her shoulder, bringing her back from the dream. She sat up fast, her gaze finding Elliot even in the darkness. His eyebrows, slanted downward, as he looked at her with concern, even though she knew he couldn't see her.

"Mel? You okay?"

She tried to catch her breath. "My mind is doing screwed up things. I... I may need to get myself to a healer. Or have Ava make me something to drink that will help or something. I took the attack and twisted it. This time I died."

He floated over her until he could sit down on the side of the bed next to her, more toward the center. "That's awful. I know bad dreams quite well. I've had a number of them myself, and I don't have any easy solution. I heard you cry out, and I came. I hope that's okay."

It was more than okay. "You needed a lawyer and now you have a wreck living in your house."

"Stop." He pulled her against his side. "I've had to do nothing but take and take and take from people since the curse got me. It's nice to be able to help someone else. Plus, there is the whole lusting after me all through your childhood as some kind of sexual fantasy thing."

Her cheeks heated up. "I didn't put it like that."

"No, but as I expand on this story in my head to fit my own tragic need for an ego boost, I am growing the scope of your so-called crush on me."

She groaned. "Elliot... don't make me pinch you."

"Oh, go ahead, pinch away. I have clearly struck a nerve here." She didn't pinch him. Instead, she poked him once in the side. He jumped before he laughed. "Poking the blind cursed guy. I see how it is, Melanie."

The dream was gone, fled from her mind like it had never

been there at all. She was sure that was why he'd done this, thrown her crush over the top until they were both laughing. He leaned back on the headboard. "You picked this room? I always thought it was creepy. No wonder you had bad dreams in here."

"Creepy?" She looked around. "I find it just the opposite. Warm. Inviting."

He scrunched up his face. "The little girl—what was her name?—my mother always knew it—oh, Andrea—she died in here. Like maybe in this bed."

Melanie doubted it was the same bed. Magic could do a lot but not preserve a mattress that long. Plus, it was a king-sized bed. There was no way the twelve-year-old girl had one of those back then.

"Do we know how Andrea died? And I'd like to point out the hypocrisy of you finding this room creepy when you are apparently being visited by ghosts in your room."

He tugged on her arm, and she moved closer to him. It should have been strange to do so but it wasn't. After a second of readjusting, she lay with her head on his chest. Beneath her ear, his heart beat slow and steady. "I can be as hypocritical as I want on this matter. This room is creepy. I think she got sick. They called it magic poisoning back then. Who knows what that means? Scary room."

It really wasn't. There were other parts of the house that might be called that but not here. No, this was a safe spot. "Thanks for coming in here, waking me, and this."

He nodded. "I get to be your hero for five minutes."

"I didn't say hero." Still, she gave in to the need and snuggled closer against him. "You put that word in my mouth."

"Hero." He smiled broadly. "I'm taking it and owning it. You think I'm your hero, Mel."

No wonder he'd always been so popular with women. Elliot flirted whether he meant to or not. The gossip pages had once been filled with him. "Sorry, you must have me mixed up with another woman. We could go pull out the news clippings and see which one you must be thinking of from the write ups of your dating life."

Now it was his turn to groan. "Most of that was overblown."

"Ah, your honor, please take note that Mr. Boothe said most not all. That therefore means some of it must have been accurate."

He tugged her slightly tighter. "Guilty. I plead guilty. I did some stupid things I wouldn't do again. I hurt some people, emotionally. I wasn't always as clear as I should have been about my intentions. I learned to be very upfront about things. Like, hey, I'd like to hang out and have a good time, but I'm never getting married, never soul binding, and kids are out of the picture entirely. I think in those early days, when my antics were written about, I was hurting pretty badly watching my father go downhill, and I was just generally a jackass in my early twenties, not thinking about the future."

"I'm not here to judge you. I'm… guilty of many mistakes. A woman is dead because of me." It hurt to say that aloud. "If I'd been more careful this whole mess didn't have to happen."

He ran his hand through her hair. "My first instinct is to say to you, Melanie, that that's not true. You didn't cause this. But… I don't know what you did or didn't do. If there were steps you should have taken and didn't, that will be hard to live with. I am sorry this is happening to you. More than I can say. I do know for a fact that you didn't make Peter Evans kill anyone, you didn't cause that woman to marry him despite his very well-known history. You didn't hire an assassin. If intent matters, and I think that it does, this isn't on you."

The heaviness of everything descended on her. "I'm going to cry. I won't do it on you."

"My shirt can be dried. Don't move. Stay right there."

She didn't know how Elliot had turned out to be just who she needed in this mess, but she'd be forever grateful he was there.

ing, I wouldn't move.

the night carried me down here. I wasn't hurt.

She didn't know what I said to me, quickly in fact who

because in the lines the head on her or grandmother was

them.

CHAPTER 6

*M*elanie woke up slowly. She was stiff like she'd lain in one place too long. It took her a minute to recall where she was or who she was with, since the first thing she became aware of was the sound of someone's heartbeat against her ear and the easy breaths he took in and out. The night before rushed at her, and she remembered it all at once. The bad dream. The emotions. The crying herself to sleep against his chest.

He smelled good. That was a funny thought, but the most pressing in her mind. It was morning, and he still had the scent of whatever soap he'd used the day before on his skin. She lifted her head, fully expecting him to be awake and annoyed. She'd cried herself to sleep on him, and he'd been stuck all night.

Instead, his eyes were closed, and from the looks of it, he was actually asleep. She stared at him for a long second. He almost never slept, but he was right now. She laid her head back down. Well, she wouldn't move and wake him. Besides, how many times in her life was she going to get to lie still with Elliot Boothe?

She closed her eyes and just breathed. Eventually, he squirmed. A pained expression crossed his face before his lids popped open, revealing the white underneath. For just a second, right there on his face, was such pain it stole her breath. He didn't have up any guards yet, and she'd never seen him so exposed before.

He rubbed his eyes with one hand and squeezed her back gently with the other. She hugged him, and he smiled, the mask clearly fixing itself back over his face. "Morning. Or I think it is. Is it morning?"

She cleared her throat. "It's morning. Thank you for basically letting me sob all over you and pass out on top of you all night."

He moved his hand to run it through her hair. "I haven't slept in nights but then you snuggled up and you were warm. It was... soothing to have you so close, to feel like there was another human being to get through the night with. I passed right out. I should be thanking you."

That was the sweetest thing, and if she really did help him rest, then she was glad. "I can go make us a celebratory breakfast for both of us sleeping peacefully, and then I'm going to tackle your project. But not because I'm your lawyer, I think that ship has sailed, but because I'm your friend."

He took her hand, bringing it to his mouth to kiss it. She shuddered. Why had he done that? They'd cuddled but this was... different.

"If I wasn't this mess, this shell of who I used to be, I wouldn't just be your friend."

Her heart pounded hard. She forced herself to swallow. "You don't even know if you'd find me physically attractive."

"Oh, I'm sure I would. Long, dark chestnut brown hair. Don't be too impressed. That is what Edward told me the first day. Big brown eyes." He ran his fingers down her arm.

"Sun kissed, tan skin. I can feel the rest of you. It's not a pretty way to figure things out, but it works. You have beautiful, smooth features." He touched her cheek as he'd done several times, running his thumb down her nose this time. "And not to put too fine a point on it, but your breasts have been pushed up against me all night. I'm pretty damned sure I'd find you attractive. I already do. Like a teenager, I've got morning wood going on here."

Her cheeks flamed so hot she was sure she would be bright red if she looked in the mirror. She'd have been lying if she didn't at least admit to herself that she wanted him, white eyes and all. "What would you say to me now if you weren't cursed? If you weren't in this situation?"

The corners of his lips curved to an almost smile. "I'd say in my most placating voice something like this." He cleared his throat. "I can't commit to you, Melanie. It's not that I wouldn't want to. It's just that I know ahead of time that I can't possibly. But if you wanted to have a great time, to spend time knowing that we will part ways and move on with it, then I'd be game. If that isn't what you want, then I get that, too."

She touched his lips with her fingertips before she could overthink what she was going to do. There were a million reasons to not kiss him and just one to do it. She listened to that one. She wanted him.

When her mouth met his, he didn't hesitate. He kissed her back. They'd spent the night pressed to each other. Maybe this was just hormonal, a result of pure need. She didn't really care the reasons. He pulled her closer until she lay on top of him for a second before he rolled them both over, his body pinning her to the bed.

He kissed and kissed her. Melanie lost herself to the feeling. With his hand in her hair and their bodies pressed so close together, if they'd been undressed, she wasn't at all sure she'd have been able to tell where one of them started and the other ended. Her heart raced with excitement. Yes, she wanted this.

Elliot pulled back to smile down at her. "I didn't bring you here to do this. It wasn't some... plan. I just want you, Melanie. I don't have a right to want anything right now, but I do."

She kissed his chin. "I'm not complaining, Elliot. I've heard your speech. I won't get attached." Or more attached. "I want you."

"It's hard not being able to see that. There are cues I could miss. Say no if that's what you want and this stops. I..."

A loud ringing noise sounded and Elliot stopped. "Someone is here. An approved someone but the house is letting me know someone has arrived. It's got to be Edward."

"Sir?" Edward's voice sounded in the hall, and Elliot sighed.

He grinned down at her. "I'll go say good morning to him. He'll get worried if I don't. Can we pick this back up later? Please. I'd much rather be in here, but I don't want him to come looking."

She touched the side of his face. "Probably better if we both took a breath anyway. I need to shower and I need some clothes..."

He nodded. "I'll get that taken care of for you. Don't breathe too much. You're mine alone tonight. I hope. Unless you say no."

She wouldn't be saying no. "Go see Edward."

He rose from the bed and very obviously had to adjust his pants. "Fuck. I'm like a teenager."

Melanie leaned back on her elbows. One good thing about his not being able to see her was that he had no idea how she ogled him right now. Although, maybe he did, because he winked at her. She lay back down. Men were men, even if they couldn't see you, she supposed.

* * *

THE SHOWER CALMED her raging hormones, and she emerged from her bedroom—not her bedroom, the butterfly room, she had to remember that—with a smile on her face. The kitchen was empty but stocked with everything she could need. She magically whipped up some coffee before she set out to start this day on a better foot than the last few had gone.

A pop sounded, and she turned around expecting to see Lawson. At the same time, the house howled. It was a startling, angry noise, and she covered her ears instantly, dropping her coffee, which might have shattered into a million pieces if she hadn't also magically stopped it from hitting the ground. A man stood in front of her, his eyes wide, his own ears covered.

"I'm an Enforcer. I'm Danny. Lawson sent me to check on you."

The house stopped wailing as Elliot stormed into the room waving his hand. "Then you should ring the fucking bell. It'll alert us that someone is coming and then give us time to decide if the person is safe. I told Lawson this. Why didn't he send you that way?"

Danny sighed. "He likes to test things. Obviously, I'm the security test today. Sorry. It was hard to get through. Took me an hour to make the transference and only then because I'm an Enforcer."

Elliot sighed. "The Enforcer arrogance is not exaggerated. If I'd wanted to, I could have killed you. The house is magically set up to do that."

It was? She swallowed. Not that she could pop anywhere, but she'd be sure to ring the doorbell, always. Melanie set the coffee cup down on the table magically and took a deep breath. She steeled her back. Clearly, this wasn't an emergency or Lawson would have come himself or sent Stefan. Neither one of them would have taken an hour to get through.

Or they'd have rung the doorbell.

"Hi, Danny. How can we help you?"

He smiled at her, his gaze catching hers, and she noticed him noticing her, the way that men did. She'd magically cleaned her clothes but that was never as good as changing them. Her hair was still wet, and she hadn't done it up, although she would when it was less damp. Truth was, un-put-together felt more vulnerable than when she was dressed for battle at work.

She crossed her arms over her chest and waited for him to speak. Just because he'd given off the I'm attracted to you vibe didn't mean he would have to follow it up by saying or doing anything about it.

"Hi, Melanie, ah, sorry, yeah... Lawson sent me. You have lots of people trying to reach you. We've been intercepting it to make sure it's safe. But I've brought it to you now. If you want to answer and send it back, Lawson set up a location that will make it safe for you to do so. And we wanted to make sure you had everything you needed."

She smiled, taking the paper from him. It wasn't the same as voices or images, but she'd take the contact however it came through. "Thanks, I'm doing fine. How are things going? Have you found Peter Evans, or if you have, do you have anything you can use to actually charge him?"

Elliot walked further in the room. "They're Enforcers. You're thinking like a lawyer. If Lawson catches Peter, he doesn't need anything legal to take him, Mel. He'll be gone, period."

Danny smiled. "That is very true. We're not so much concerned with due process when it comes to these kind of witching criminals. He's not a petty thief. This is murder and attempted murder using magical assassins."

This part of the Enforcer system had always bugged her. People deserved a trial. But she was bathing in hypocrisy because the idea of Peter just vanishing worked for her, too. She rubbed the back of her neck.

"Well, okay then. I... I'm not in an arguing mood. Thanks for coming by and bringing me the messages."

Danny cleared his throat. "Hey, you know I could check with Lawson, but I'd bet it would be safe if you wanted to get out of here for a while if you went with me. I could take you out, keep you safe, and bring you back."

Elliot visibly jolted, and Melanie had to control herself from wincing. This again. She realized this was a highbrow problem to have and that there might come a time when she missed having the attention of men wherever she went. But right now she was on the verge of a headache, trying to figure out things for her future, making out with Elliot even though that could go nowhere, and basically trying not to spend all of her time either asleep or crying.

It wasn't the time for this.

"Thank you so much for wanting to take me out. That's very sweet. But I'm one big goop of baggage. I can assure you that you don't want to date me. I'm such a mess." She smiled. "Consider yourself lucky you missed out on this mess. Thanks again."

Danny cleared his throat. "Oh, okay. Well, let me know if you change your mind."

He popped away. Elliot put his hand on the wall with a clunk. "A big goop of baggage?"

She waved her hand and groaned. "I may not be at my most articulate."

"It's really amazing. I've been with you with two single men now and both of them have asked you out. Does that happen to you everywhere? Do people stop you on the street?"

With her messages in her hand, she passed by him, patting him on the arm. "Well, you had your tongue in my mouth just this morning so maybe I am irresistible."

"No argument there." He grabbed onto her hand before she could pull it away. "I am going to ask you something totally unreasonable."

Well, that was the strangest introduction to a question she'd ever heard. "Um, okay."

"Don't say yes while you're living here. Can you? I have no rights to anything with you. I've already told you that I told women regularly there was no future and you know better than most why that can't be. I think most women thought the curse was something funny, not real, or something they could break like a reverse Sleeping Beauty. You know what is going to happen to me. For the first time ever, I don't have to explain to a woman I like why I'm... ultimately unavailable. I won't do to someone what my father did to my mother and me. I won't take them down with me. And... you don't seem afraid of my eyes."

She squeezed their linked hands. "Elliot..."

He interrupted. "Let me finish. I know I'm rambling. I like having you here more than I should. I want to... wow I'm just going to say it... I want to make you come. Over and over. And while you're staying here, I don't want to think of you with anyone else. That's selfish and not fair. I'm still asking. Saying no won't change anything between us. I... I'm just asking."

She leaned her head onto his shoulder. "I can barely

figure out anything right now. All I know is I want to be in your bed tonight. How's that? I don't want to date anyone. I'm not lying when I tell them that I'm too much for them. It takes a real kind of personality to deal with me, and I'm tired of trying with men who can't."

He scrunched up his face. 'What do you mean by that?"

"I don't want to do this right now. I'm trying to avoid crying or sleeping. This topic makes me want to do both. Come on. I'm going to look at my messages and then tackle your boxes. I like to feel busy."

Edward rushed into the room. "I was on the other side of the property dealing with the recycling. What's wrong? What's going on?"

Elliot didn't drop her hand, instead he squeezed tighter. "Well, it's a good thing we're not dead, Edward. No, seriously, don't worry about it. Security isn't your job. I realize we have some extenuating circumstances here. A lot of them. Thanks for checking."

She tugged on their linked fingers, a motion that Edward definitely noted, and took him back to the study. Elliot wanted to make her come. She could hardly breathe for thinking about that. Yes, she was in favor of that, too. Even if everything was a little fucked up.

* * *

SHE'D PLACE money on Elliot's mind not being on what they were doing, which was okay because Melanie had gotten pretty good at determining what he'd think they should keep and what they should discard. He was sort of humming to himself and turning at every noise he heard. She wasn't entirely focused herself. In between boxes, she read her messages.

Her friends had seen the news before the Enforcers had

shut down the stories, and they were worried. She'd answered five before she had to get back to thinking about something else. Too many answers about what happened without actually saying what happened were making her itchy. She needed to send a message where she talked and didn't just spell cast a response to her parents, Ava, and Eleanor. The last two had been there to see what happened and needed a lot of reassurance. Her mom and dad were just worried, as parents were prone to be.

She side-eyed Elliot, not sure exactly what he was doing. He seemed to be tapping his foot to a song she couldn't hear anywhere and every so often he'd bite down on his lip. What was he hearing?

She spelled a box out of the room to the discarded, finished shelf in the garage when she saw the man. Melanie stumbled backward hitting the desk. Had she really seen what she thought she did? Yes, there was a man staring in the window.

"What is it?" Elliot looked up at her, stopping the drum rhythm he was doing. "You okay?"

"There's someone outside the window."

He rubbed his nose. "Not possible. No one can get on the grounds that we don't let in except the Enforcers, and even then, I've taken steps to make it harder."

"Okay, except he's staring right at me. Dark hair, glasses, overalls."

Elliot's smile was fast. "That's Alan. He's the ghost gardener."

She walked over to the window. "That man that I can see as clear as day standing right there staring at us is... a ghost? No, that's not possible. It's safe to go outside right?"

He stretched out his feet. "As long as you stay on the property you're golden."

She rushed out of the room and down the hall to the

front door. Making her way outside, she ran to the window, abruptly stopping short. Yes, there was the ghost gardener. No, it couldn't just be. There weren't ghosts running around. Ancient witches that somehow managed not to die and tried to possess Eleanor, okay. That was magic related but this was just... no.

Besides, she had lived here for years and never seen any ghosts. How was this possible?

The gardener moved from the window and started walking through what at some time must have been a garden. Elliot's mother had loved to keep the house beautiful with things growing all around it. But now those things were gone. As he looked like he dug in the dirt, he wasn't actually touching any plants or doing anything.

It was possible this was Elliot playing a joke. Not that she could fathom how he did this. A projection spell? Still, she didn't think so. He didn't seem to waste power. She reached out and her hand went right through the ghost.

She darted backward as the gardener looked up at her. "It should be a good growth this year, ma'am."

Okay. This was happening. "How are you here?"

He didn't answer her but looked down at the ground. Elliot walked up behind her. "He doesn't really talk. I mean, other than what he says about the growth. He's not communicative."

She swallowed, leaning back on him when his arms came around her. He touched her like it was the most natural thing in the world and maybe that's why it felt like it was. "How did I not see these things my whole childhood?"

"I don't have an answer for that. Let's go ask your parents. Come on. He'll vanish soon. I used to sit out here when I was a kid and watch him. My father apparently did the same thing. Generations of us communicating with ghosts."

She let him lead her toward the house. "I have to say that freaked me out. It really did."

"He's harmless. They all are. Even the one in the attic that we can all hear but can't ever find. It's just an... unusual part of the house."

That apparently she had missed her entire childhood. She yawned. "Sorry. Thought I was doing pretty well."

He squeezed her hand. "You are. Not one tear yet today."

"Well, the day's not over. I could end up sobbing."

He kissed her cheek. "Only in pleasure today. You'll see."

"I want to get through another box before I pass out."

The best laid plans. She must have fallen right out on the desk when she sat down to organize it because that was the last thing she remembered. She woke up on the couch, her feet on Elliot's lap. He seemed to be listening to something with headphones on. When she moved, he took them off and smiled at her.

"Are you up?" He kept his voice low, which was considerate if she'd still been sleeping.

"Sorry about that. Guess when it hits me... it takes me down."

He grinned at her. "I might not have known you were asleep if you hadn't started snoring."

Melanie sat up fast. "I did not. Oh, wow. I've never heard that I snore but..."

He squeezed her foot. "I'm joking with you. You were perfectly quiet. Hungry?"

Her stomach growled in response. "I guess so."

As she stood up, a crack of thunder sounded outside so loudly it shook the house. She grabbed onto Elliot, and he laughed. "That's a loud one. I never think of us as getting rain this time of year."

The sound of the rain followed fast, hitting the roof. Now this, she remembered. These old houses didn't hide the noise like the modern apartments did. Thunder clapped again, and she rubbed her arms. "I've never cared for heavy downpours. The tsunami that came out of nowhere didn't help things either."

"Oh, right. A few years ago. Heard that was a weather witch who got out of hand."

It was Ava's father, but Mel wasn't going to share that. She was good at keeping people's secrets.

Elliot suddenly pointed at her. "I have a memory of you. It just hit me like a ton of bricks. You were tiny, a toddler. You'd come into the house with your mom; she was supervising some change in the dining room, I think. It was storming, and you were crying your eyes out. She'd left you for a moment so I sat with you on the floor until you stopped. She came running back, told me they thought you really hated the weather."

Melanie wasn't certain how she felt about the man she wanted to have sex with remembering her as a toddler, but it was cute he had that memory. "I do hate storms." She walked up to him, pressing her body against his. "So distract me."

Edward should be done for the day, and if he wasn't, well, he could just keep his interruptions to himself. Elliot's mouth was soft as he met her own. His arms came around her, strong, like they could keep out any storm that wanted to come near her, even with the curse he carried around every second of the day.

"Melanie, I don't want to disappoint you. I need you to tell me what you want and don't want, okay? And if you like or don't like something."

She kissed his chin. "I promise to make it very, very obvious."

Elliot floated both of them into the air. She wrapped her arms around his neck. "You are so incredible. That's not a good enough word. How did this happen? How did you come into my life during this… impossible time?"

She was done talking, even though his words were amazingly sweet. She kissed him again, letting him know in no uncertain terms exactly what she wanted.

Melanie M.

CHAPTER 7

$\mathcal{M}$elanie had never been kissed the way that Elliot did. It wasn't so much that their lips met together as much as it was that he owned her mouth. She followed where he led, not wanting anything to disrupt this feeling. Her body was on fire and they hadn't done anything more than kiss.

He pulled back, his thumbs caressing her face, tracing the slope of her nose. "You're okay doing this in the study? I can find us a bed and be civilized about this."

There was nothing remotely civilized about how she was feeling right then. "The couch. The floor. The top of the desk. Floating in the air. I want you, Elliot. However it happens."

He pressed his forehead to hers. "Why? I'm such... I'm half of what I should be right now."

"You're so sexy, Elliot. White eyed or not. Don't doubt that."

His smile was ridiculously huge. "Well, you have been crushing on me your whole life."

"I didn't say that."

She liked how he teased her. Melanie wasn't sure that

anyone had ever really done that before. Her family and friends weren't teasers. There was something so... intimate about it. Even if she found out he did it to everyone he knew, it would still feel personal to her.

He went back to kissing her, and she lost herself to it. Her head felt lighter, her body on fire. He kissed her all over her face. "I should be seducing you, taking you out to eat, the theater, vacations." He pushed her hair off her forehead. "I shouldn't be asking you to do this in my study when you can never leave my house."

She led him over to the couch. "I don't need seduction. I almost died this week, and you're going through hell. Let's just take our time when we can."

"Agreed." He kissed her cheek. "That doesn't mean I don't think you should have all of those things." She drew him to her, and Elliot shuddered. "Melanie."

She did love how he said her name. Melanie waved her hand, and his shirt vanished. He laughed, a great sound. Nestled up against him like this with only better things to come, she didn't even care that every so often thunder banged outside, slightly shaking the house.

Melanie kissed a path across his chest, stopping right over his heart. She pressed a gentle kiss there. He had a huge heart, giving, and almost never asking for anything in return, except, in her case that she not date anyone else while she stayed at his house. How could he have thought she would want to?

Her own shirt vanished. "You're not the only one, Mel, who can use magic to get what they want."

She almost never wore a bra. Her figure had always been on the slender side with her boobs matching the rest of her. Melanie took his hand and led it to her breast. He flared his nostrils, which made her grin. Elliot couldn't see her breasts but that didn't mean they didn't affect him. He pressed his mouth on her shoulder, and he stroked her nipples, bringing them to a peak. They ached, and she smiled. Wow, how she loved this painful need.

He moved to her other breast, and she kissed his chest. He breathed hard, kissing up her neck. It should have been awkward being sort of all over the place and on the edge of the couch, but it wasn't.

He bent over, kissing her nipple before he took it in his mouth. Elliot sucked hard. She cried out, and he let go. "Too much?"

"No. I really like it. Sorry, it just took me by surprise."

He shook his head. "I'd do anything to see you, Melanie, but since I can't wish that into existence, I've got to ask you while I am learning your delicious noises. Don't get embarrassed. I don't have your face to tell me if that is good or bad. I'll be a fast study."

"Guess that means we'll just have to do this a lot so that we can both learn each other."

He smiled. "Sounds like a plan."

He was hard. She could feel it through his pants. Melanie reached down, stroking him. He moaned, bringing her nipple farther into his mouth. She couldn't decide what she liked more, the fact that she could get that reaction from him or what he was doing to her breast.

A touch of magic took his pants and briefs away. He laughed and did the same to her. Next time, she'd undress him with her hands. There was something nice about that, too. But she wanted him and patience had never been her forte.

He pushed her backward until she lay beneath him on the couch. Her heart rate sped up. What was he going to do? Elliot kissed down her body, stopping just before her pussy to lay kisses on both of her thighs.

"Elliot..." She'd never been great at accepting oral sex as much as she loved giving it.

He lifted his white gaze as though he would meet her own if he could. "I hear nerves in that voice, Mel. I really want to give you pleasure like this. Trust me?"

She leaned back on the couch. "I have a control issue. Yes, I'll... try. It isn't that I don't want to. I tend to just not be able to relax."

He held out his hand. "Take my hand."

That seemed a strange request given what they were about to do, but Melanie did as he said and linked their fingers together. He kissed on the outside of her pussy again. This time squeezing her fingers when he did before slipping his tongue inside of her. She cried out, and he held her fingers tighter.

There was something sort of... grounding about it. Elliot found his way quickly to her clit without needing instruction —impressive considering he couldn't see—and soon she was panting. Why was this working this time?

What did it matter? Elliot was gifted with that tongue. She gripped onto the couch with her other hand. It wasn't long before she was moaning, filling the room with the sounds of her pleasure. Her mind tried to twist away. She'd never liked being conscious of herself. It went against all the other ways she always felt confident and sure, but there it was.

Elliot lifted his head. "You taste so good, Mel. I could do this all day."

His voice brought her back to the moment. It helped that he squeezed her hand. She'd never known she needed a tactile experience to keep her present. He pressed his tongue back on her clit, and she exploded. Her back arched, and she practically came off the couch. Pleasure rushed through her, and he pressed their fingers together so hard that for a second, her hand ached. He sighed, pulling back.

"You just gave me such a gift." He smiled at her. "Thank you."

She'd given him a gift? No, it was the other way around. "Come here, Elliot."

She waved her hand, which gave him a magical push toward her. He laughed before catching himself on the couch. Elliot said he wasn't good at being blind, but he did manage himself pretty well. She'd probably have fallen on her face, and she needed to do a better job of remembering that when she played with him like this.

Melanie kissed him, putting her entire soul into it. Yes, she couldn't get attached. Yes, this would end when the man after her was caught. Yes, he was cursed and would be gone but... she really was crazy about him. For this one moment, she was going to let herself feel that fully and not worry about it.

There would be later to wish she'd protected herself.

She reached for his cock, and he shook his head. "No. I'll come over your fingers. You make me feel like I'm fifteen. Next time. Now, if it's okay, I'd like to be inside of you."

Was it okay? Yes, it was seriously okay. "Absolutely."

He kissed her chin. "I've had the healers make it so I can't father a child. A magical vasectomy if you will. But I'd like to make sure you're covered birth control-wise anyway. It's important to me that I not leave anyone here to inherit this curse. Even by mistake."

She nodded, but he couldn't see that. "Absolutely. I'll take care of that right now."

"Or I can." He smoothed his hand over her skin, a warm feeling following the sensation. "I'd like to. I want to take care of you."

She blinked. "Are you real? Or have I somehow made you up in my head?"

His smile was huge as he spelled her birth control so she wouldn't get pregnant. It felt like someone had flooded her with gentle heat. "Better than your crush?"

Melanie groaned. "I am going to regret ever telling you that."

"Don't. It gives me an enormous amount of happiness." Elliot kissed her again before he pressed her legs apart. Skin on skin, she could feel his arousal against her leg. "You're still wet."

She bit down on his earlobe. "Well, considering how you just made me come, that isn't surprising."

"True." He pressed himself inside of her. It had been a little while since Melanie was intimate with anyone. Elliot wasn't small, and it took her body a few moments to adjust to the sheer size of him. He moved slowly, letting her catch up, and finally, he was fully sheathed inside of her.

He pressed their foreheads together. "I should be asking you if you're for real. I might be hallucinating this whole thing."

She wrapped her arms around him. "No. This is real."

They moved together like they'd been doing this forever. None of the jerky, trying to figure each other out feelings of a new lover. She raised her hips, and he followed her in the joining. In and out. Elliot changed the thrust of his hips to rub against her clit, and she was lost. She started moaning so loud she drowned out the thunder, and soon she was biting on his shoulder in some last ditch effort to hold back the explosion he drew out of her.

"Don't fight it, Mel." He kissed her all over her face. "Give in. I've got you."

As though his words gave her permission, she lost it in an orgasm that rocked her to her very soul. He followed her fast after she did, coming on a sigh of her name. It was the sweetest moment she'd ever had sexually.

And when the tears came, the fact that he couldn't see them was helpful. She turned her head just slightly and brushed them aside. He didn't need to know that this had meant something to her when it had been so clear that there couldn't be anything more than friendship between them.

Putting on her best pleasant voice, she spoke. He hadn't lifted his head off her shoulder, and she wondered if he'd fallen asleep there on top of her, still slightly hard inside of her core. "That's quite a storm out there."

He lifted his head. "Are we going to small talk the weather?" Elliot kissed her lips. "You okay? Did I hurt you?"

Oh, he had to mean the tears. "Sometimes I cry when I... come. Sorry."

That had never happened before, not that she would tell him that. She was still wrecked from the attack. She'd go with that. He tilted his head slightly as though he considered what she said. Finally, he nodded. "That was incredible."

"It was," she had to agree. "Are you okay?"

He shot his eyebrows skyward on his forehead. "Am I? Never better. Come here. Let's change places. You on top of me. You're tinier than I am. You won't crush me while we cuddle."

She let him flip them over, and then she settled down to lie on him. Melanie hadn't contacted her parents, and she was hungry, but all of that could wait. How many chances in life would she get to snuggle with Elliot?

He ran his hands through her hair. When he spoke, it was in a low voice. "I'd do anything to see you, and I haven't felt that way in a long time. I thought I had sort of accepted things."

She kissed his chest. "I'm sorry. You stay so happy and pleasant. You are such an inspiration."

His answer was a hard laugh. "I'm a mess. I'm glad I'm faking it so well."

So they had that in common. Both of them hid their inner chaos from the world. Her mind drifted to other messes she was involved in. It was impossible to put off thinking of Peter Evans. He'd killed his wife and Melanie was supposed to have protected her as best she could under the law. The Enforcers hadn't gotten to her in time, hadn't found out why she had agreed to a loveless soul binding. Now they'd never know.

"What would make a person decide to tie themselves to Peter Evans? To share a soul with a man who had multiple divorces in a world where we so rarely do that. We have a ceremony, a spell binding of our souls. I'll probably never know what that's like, but it does something to people. I've seen it. They are changed afterward, better—if you can believe it. What does it mean that he keeps undoing it and why would he?"

Elliot chewed on his bottom lip. "I've met him a few times. Benefits for libraries. Musicals. He's an asshole. A rich douche bag. Why anyone would want to soul bind with him even if it was real, I don't know." He rubbed his face. "That's not a good answer. I don't know. I'm sorry, Melanie. Like you I've only ever seen it from a distance. I don't know what happens with the soul sharing, and I don't know how not being in love affects that."

"I'm going to get answers. I have to. It'll eat me alive otherwise."

He kissed her palm. "I don't blame you. Hey, you never did tell me what you thought of the Bomber play?"

Oh, yes she'd been a little distracted. "I got a little busy."

"True, and I wasn't thinking about it either, but now I am. What did you think?"

His heart beat strong beneath her ear. "I loved it. Very

moving. If you want to go, we should arrange that when it's not dangerous for me. Or you don't have to babysit me. Or, you know, before it closes. You can go."

"No need for that. Which part made you cry?"

Her something-was-off radar turned on. "If you haven't seen it how will you know which part I'm talking about?"

He scrunched up his nose. "Let's say I'm familiar with the show."

"How can that be?" She drummed her fingers on his chest.

"Maybe I'm not the lazy playboy everyone thinks I am. Maybe I had a career that no one knew about and will never know about until after I'm dead."

Realization hit her hard. "You're Bomber."

He nodded. "Guilty."

She sat up fast, and he groaned as she put weight on his legs for a second before she scooted off. "You are the hidden author of the plays and musicals that are considered the greatest work of the witching world in this generation."

His grin was huge. "Oh I like that one. Who said that about me?"

"Elliot, for goodness sake. People should know this about you."

He shook his head fast. "Not till I'm dead, Mel. Otherwise it's just the Cursed Family they talk about. My family. What happens to us? Not the work itself. Don't tell anyone. I'm trusting you."

She sighed. "Of course I won't tell anyone. You're my friend."

"That means a lot to me." He sat up next to her and kissed her shoulder. "I realized when this happened that I don't have a lot of friends. Lots of people around wanting things. They like the rich, they like the money. They liked the trips and going places. The wine. I don't know. I'm not sure I took the time to really develop lasting friendships. I knew I'd likely check out early. Your family was my family. That's why I called them and that's why when they told me what you were up to I called you. I'm really glad I did."

He was Bomber. "You write beautiful words. I'm not surprised now that I know. You do have a tendency to say very profound things."

"Aw, you are so good for my ego. I can hardly stand it." He winked at her. "Thank you for that. Seriously. I made the choice to not have a family. Not that any woman I met ever inspired me to want to. I know that sounds awful. I think I might be a little... selfish and self-centered. I didn't feel whatever it is that you're supposed to feel. I digress. The point is I'm glad I'm leaving something behind that was meaningful to people."

She didn't know what to say to most of that and so teasing him seemed the only choice. "Not one of those blondes I've seen you on the news with inspired you to walk down the aisle?"

"Oh, you've seen me on the gossip shows?" He kissed her hand. "And what's with the problem with the blondes? I like brunettes, too, Mel. As you know."

He didn't really know if he'd have found her attractive or not. That really was neither here nor there. "I'm getting dressed and composing a message to my parents. I might find some food, too. Edward should be gone now, right?"

"Long gone. I'm sorry I used him as an excuse this morning to delay this."

His words startled her. "Did you do that because you didn't want to do this?"

Elliot rose, spelling his clothes back on. She dressed herself as well and waited for him to talk. "I meant what I said when I said I wanted to wine and dine you. I felt like... like I wasn't really within my rights to do this. I decided to believe you when you said you wanted this, too. You are okay with everything, right?"

She forced herself to smile because it would help her to sell it. "I'm a grown woman. I'm good at doing casual sex without expectations of walking down the aisle and soul binding. You're my friend. I never expected to have you in my life at all. I'll take this. Okay?"

He took her hand in his. "Okay, Mel."

She really hoped he believed her. Besides, he'd told her the truth. There had never been a woman who had inspired him to want forever. She wouldn't have been different even if every bit of circumstances were changed. The girls who thought they could change a forever bachelor drove her crazy. Mostly, if you listened closely, people did a pretty good job of telling you who they were. Elliot had never hidden himself. For all his gentle understanding, he didn't want forever for very good reasons. And if he'd never been cursed, they'd never have been here together anyway. There were no scenarios when he returned her infatuation.

They walked together to the dining room where she intended to send her parents a recorded message they could watch, showing them she was okay. A loud noise above their head that wasn't the storm caught her attention. It sounded like a bang. She stopped moving to stare upward.

"Oh, that's the faceless ghost."

She blinked. "The what?"

"That's what my mother called him. We have a ghost in the attic. He's never seen, but it has to be him. Or her, I guess. Just one of the spirits in the house."

She shivered. "I have to tell you I am so glad I never saw or heard one the whole time I was a child here."

"That is weird that you didn't." He shrugged. "They're just anomalies in the house that shields the Cursed Family from the world."

No, that didn't make any sense. She'd gone her whole life and never heard another witch tell one word about a ghost. Settling herself down in the living room, she sent Mitchell a note asking him if he knew anything about ghosts.

She turned her attention to her parents. With a swish of her hand, she started to record herself. The magic would place her image and what she said onto the paper they'd receive. Just as she started speaking the attic banged again.

Melanie gritted her teeth. "Hi Mom and Dad, sorry if I sound funny. I'm fine. Doing really well here. I am encountering ghosts and hearing things. Elliot says you are fully aware of them, but somehow I don't remember seeing them when I was little. Anyway, I just wanted to tell you that I am well and will be until the Enforcers catch Peter Evans. You be safe. I love you."

Elliot came out from the kitchen and wrapped his arms around her from behind. "Hi, Judy and Max. I'm taking good care of your daughter and somehow we are managing to not burn the place down. Try not to worry too much. Let's ask Lawson if you can come visit."

The easy way he touched her in a video being sent to her parents should have concerned her. But if he wasn't bothered, she wasn't going to be.

As she sent off the message to Lawson's safe address, Elliot came back in, holding two plates filled with pasta. "I can make this without having to be able to see it."

"It smells great."

The banging noise sounded again. Ghosts scared her. That much was true, but like storms, she couldn't avoid this. "After dinner I'm going up there. I want to make sure your faceless ghost isn't actually a large squirrel banging around in your attic."

Elliot laughed. "Have at it. I looked a lot when I was a kid. Nothing. And always the same noise."

"Well, I am going to give it my best try. I'm good at riddling out puzzles, and you are one. So is this house." She hadn't noticed it when she was a child, being too preoccupied with Elliot himself. And then when he was out of the house and his father's health declined, she'd spent a lot of time trying not to notice what was happening. By then she'd been pretty inwardly focused, too. The situation of being not super-rich in a school where most people were had been enough to keep her attention.

Still, shouldn't she have noticed ghosts? Plural. More than one.

Elliot sat back in his chair. "Have at it, Mel. Maybe you'll solve it. You're certainly smart enough to do so."

She hadn't felt that way lately. "People smarter than me have tried to fix this. But maybe I can at least figure out who your ghost is up there."

There were too many mysteries in her life right now. Something had to start to make sense. She was going to get to the bottom of that noise. And so help her, if it was generations of rats, she was going to manage not to run screaming from the attic. Somehow. Thunder boomed, and the rain poured down. Melanie was sick of being scared. She couldn't control assassins but this she could get a grasp on.

CHAPTER 8

*M*elanie floated up to the attic. For years, Ava had seemed powerless, and it had really given Melanie an idea of how difficult things were for humans. They'd have needed a ladder to get up there. Of course, power was relative. The Enforcers could have just popped on up.

The attic was loaded with dust, and it took an illumination spell to light the place up. Her mother must never have come up here because it looked like it had been generations since anyone had cleaned the place. In fact, no one had come to clean the house since she'd been here. Edward ran things, but where was the staff? It used to take half a dozen people to run the Boothe estate.

She was going to have to ask Elliot.

In the meantime, she wandered through the attic, ducking to avoid hitting her head on some beams that were low, but otherwise seeing nothing but boxes that needed to be gone through. She sighed. There was lot more work left to do than she'd thought. With a flick of her wrist she sent them downstairs to the study. Elliot might not even know these were up here needing to be sorted.

Goosebumps broke out on her arms, and she rubbed them. Melanie swallowed before she turned around, slowly, to see what had made her heebie-jeebies stand on alert. Nothing was there. She sighed. There hadn't been anything to see the whole time she was up here.

"Find anything?" She jumped before shrieking. It took her half a second to realize it was Elliot. He shook his head at her. "Sorry, didn't mean to terrify you."

"Yes you did or you would have made some noise." She laughed. The high after being scared of something and then finding out it was nothing was like riding a human roller coaster. Up and down. Up and down. She'd only done it once, but it was the closest feeling she could relate this to.

He held up his hands. "Seriously, find anything?"

"No." She stormed over to him. "I guess you're right. There's nothing up here I can see, Bomber."

He groaned. "Are you going to call me that now?"

"Maybe. When I feel like it. Come on. I just transported a ton of boxes to the study. We have a lot more work to do."

He ran a hand up her arm. "Or we could keep ourselves occupied in other, more enjoyable ways."

The smile that crossed her face came with a surge of warmth from his words. "I love that idea. But those boxes aren't going to sort themselves. Give me two hours of organizing and I'll race you to the bedroom to spend the night in more... productive ways."

He flared his nostrils. "I take it you're never going to be able to relax if you don't get to accomplish something productive?"

"Correct." She shrugged. "What do the humans call it? I'm a type-A personality."

He took her arm. "I've spent almost no time with humans.

But they seem to like the Bomber shows. Two of them did okay on Broadway. You still haven't told me which scene made you cry."

She wrapped her arms around him. "I'm not going to. You'll just have to suffer wondering."

Two could play the teasing game.

* * *

MELANIE HAD MADE it through the second box when Elliot started to write. It was an interesting thing to watch. He couldn't see, so he spelled a pen in the air, and it must have been taking the words directly from his head onto the paper. He leaned back on the couch, and she wondered if he was even aware that he was composing at all.

It was actually sort of beautiful. She almost asked him where his ideas came from but stopped. Was that something she really wanted to know? His ideas came alive on stage, people speaking his words. If it was a conversation he overheard at the clothes store, wouldn't that somehow cheapen the experience for her? Better to see the magic of the finished work. And if he couldn't explain it, then that had to be a bit of a frustrating conversation for him to have.

She grabbed a journal. There had been several in the box and none of them interesting. The price of groceries, what his great-great-great—she couldn't keep track of how many greats—grandfather had paid the staff. But this was different. She flipped through the pages and couldn't read any of the words. What language was that?

Melanie sat down in the chair and tried to make sense of it. Some of the letters weren't even ones she recognized.

"Elliot, sorry to interrupt, but I have a question."

He lifted his eyebrows. "Not to worry." The pen in the air didn't even stop moving. "I actually multitask when I write really well. I tend to do other things. This is just how it is now because I can't see. Sorry, off track. What's going on?"

"I found a journal. The writing isn't a language I know. Did your ancestor who built this house—because that is when this box seems to have originated from—speak a different language? Everything else has been in English."

He shook his head. "Not that I know of. We founded the area. I think we spoke the common tongue. Weird. Obviously, I can't see it to make sense of it for you."

She nodded to herself. "Yep. Got it. Would it be okay if I sent it to my friend Mitchell? He's good at this sort of thing. Ancient writings are one of his fortes."

"Sure. If you think it could help know what to do with it."

Maybe it would. At the very least, if it was gibberish drawings or something, he'd know that, too. She sent it to Mitchell.

"So it's funny going through this box. Everything is well ordered. But you guys weren't always rich. It seems like he struggled for a while. I wouldn't have thought that considering this house."

Elliot got to his feet. "We owned the land but not this house. And not all of the land, if the stories are to be true. He struck it big although the details are scarce. Any info on that yet that you've found? This is just what I was hoping to uncover for posterity. I figured someone might like to know that. His son was the first one cursed so it was always the irony. We were rich, everything we invested doubling and tripling, like we couldn't fail. Well, everyone but me. I never touched the money. Left it doing whatever it did in the accounts my father created for it. It's still earning now but not thanks to me."

"Nothing yet, but I'll keep looking. Guess it was good luck I went to the attic." She bit down on her lip. "I was always in awe of all of this, your house, the way your parents got to live. I swore someday I'd have my own fortune. And I did before I got stupid and blew it all."

Elliot walked over to her, the paper and pen floating down to the desk. "What do you mean?"

"I was earning hand over fist. Your father taught me some of his investment strategies. I worked for a law firm that specialized in making the rich richer. I was going to show all those people who treated me like less than in school that I wasn't to be discounted. But then one day it wasn't enough... I had to suddenly go out on my own. No one does that anymore. Once again I was going to show everyone. I've blown through my savings. I am going to have to ask my old boss for my job back." She rubbed her eyes. "I'm exhausted even thinking about it."

He wrapped her into his arms. "You tried. There's no failure in that. The failure would have been in not trying. My first three shows didn't get picked up anywhere. They were awful. I get how it feels to not... make it. But you will. I believe in you. There's something so strong and steady about your energy, Melanie. I can't see you, but even I can tell you're brilliant. Your mind works fast, it snaps to decisions. And who tormented you in school?"

If her mind worked fast, his was supersonic speed. "Everyone who wasn't Ava and Mitchell. Even Lawson and I used to fight. He was in the same boat as me. You'd have thought we could have been friends, but it was more like we were competitors. Stefan, too. We hardly ever spoke, but it wasn't great."

"Why were they after you for being poor? And you weren't poor. Not really. Your parents made pretty good money and you lived here."

Did he really not get it? "Elliot, my parents worked for your family. That school was filled with people who didn't hold their own staff in high regard. No, I wasn't really poor.

There are folks out there in much worse circumstances. I had everything I needed and then some. But I was the staff's child, viewed to be there as a favor to your father. I had to work three times as hard to prove my worth and even then most of them wouldn't be my friend. It's okay. I took the opportunities having that degree gave me and I ran with it. I did make two very good friends. And these days I have plenty of good people in my life. Was it so different when you went through?"

He seemed to be thinking about it. Eventually, he ran a hand over his face. "I don't know. I guess I never thought about it. I… I was pretty focused on being everyone's golden child so that I could overcome all the attention about the fact that we were cursed."

"Well, I guess we both had our burdens to bear." The difference being he was living his out, her current issues were self-imposed. She ran her hands through his hair. "We used to watch you, my friends and me, when you were in the upper school and we were in the lower. You won every sporting event, dated every pretty girl. I never knew you were putting on some kind of show. Just looked natural to me."

He kissed her. "My family funds half of the fundraising of that school. I was going to ask you, in your lawyerly role, to see to it that it continues. Now, pissed on your behalf, I want to pull their funding."

She shook her head. "Don't do that. I've benefited from it more than I was harmed."

"How are you single? I know that's a ridiculous question, but I keep asking myself that. How is there not a man in your life?"

She scrunched up her nose. "I don't lie when I tell people who ask me out that I come with a lot of baggage. I'm terrible to date. I don't do flirting well. I'm too serious in my conversation. I press people for truth when I should keep it light. I am too much. Period." She tugged on his shirt. "I think I promised you more fun things to do than this."

"I hardly even focused on this. You did all the work." He winced. "I don't mean to be flighty."

"Artists are always a little bit focused on things that aren't happening now. I don't mind it. I liked seeing how the Bomber operated."

He squeezed the back of her neck. "If we'd been the same age in school, I'd have seen to it that no one was mean to you, ever."

"That might have made it worse." She was done with this conversation. Nothing could be fixed, and even if she could go back, she wasn't sure she'd have done it differently. Her backbone seemed to be metaphorically reestablishing itself. Melanie was glad to have it back. "Come on. Let's go upstairs."

* * *

TWO ROUNDS OF LOVEMAKING LATER, Elliot snored gently next to her. He said he didn't sleep but twice now with her he certainly was. She kept his arms around her, holding him tightly. Maybe the trick was that he had to be kept physically very busy so that he simply wore himself out.

Movement caught her attention. The paper from earlier floated in the air, the pen writing on it. Did he compose in his sleep? She grinned. Did he even know that he did? The movement was small and off to the corner. She could ignore it if she wanted to.

A cold gust of wind floated over her and made her lift her head. That was weird. It wasn't cold in the house.

That was when she saw her. The ghost floated into the room. She was dressed in an old fashioned, fancy dress. At least Melanie thought it was fancy. She couldn't imagine all of that blue lace and swishy skirts being the kind of thing the woman would wear just to lounge around the house.

Melanie sighed. She was thinking about the fashion choices of ghosts and what it meant that she considered a ghost in the room relatively normal. The banging upstairs sounded again, but Mel ignored it.

All of her attention was on the woman who didn't seem to see her at all. But ghost lady certainly had eyes for Elliot. She had an almost ethereal look on her face as she walked over and seemed to touch him.

Fear coupled with anger surged through Mel. She couldn't have explained it if she'd had to, but she knew in the same way her ancestors must have known to get away from predators that she had to get that ghost away from Elliot. She swatted the air and nothing happened. The ghost didn't even seem to notice.

Still, the woman touched Elliot's cheek like she had every right to do so and it was everything she could do not to scream. The last thing she wanted was to wake Elliot, not when he struggled to sleep because of the constant bright light in his eyes. He'd lived with this ghost his whole life. Maybe Melanie needed to calm down.

She breathed through her nose and waited. After a few minutes, the ghost floated away.

This house had a ghost problem, and Melanie was going to do something about it. That was the least she could do for Elliot. He might have been fine with having them floating around, but it wasn't normal and that ghost had gotten way too close to him. Why had she done that? What did she want?

Melanie pulled the blanket farther up both of them as though she could offer him some kind of protection with the cotton quilt. He shifted slightly, pulling her tighter against him before he snored even louder. She didn't mind the noise.

That meant he was alive. The fact that she had to think about that at all made her nauseated. Why were there ghosts here, and what did that woman want with him?

She wouldn't have thought it possible, but she did eventually drift off to sleep. Melanie tried to stop herself, but the room and Elliot were warm. The place felt easier, as if she could somehow tell the ghost was gone for the night.

In his arms, she pretended she was safe and gave into the need for sleep. Tomorrow, she was going to figure out what to do about all of this crazy.

* * *

MELANIE, why don't you play with me anymore?

The sound of a little girl's voice banged around in her head as Mel came awake fast. Her heart raced, and she pulled her knees up to her forehead to try to calm down.

"You okay?" Elliot's voice was soothing as he drew her to him. The early morning light told her she hadn't been asleep very long. "Bad dreams?"

"The ghost who visited you last night freaked me out. I'm not sure what the dream was." She shook her head to clear it. "I didn't like her at all. She felt... wrong. Evil. I hate that word but there it is."

He tilted his head. "Really? She's been around always. Sometimes she talks. It's nonsensical, like the gardener, but I'd ask her things when I was young just to get an answer. She doesn't bother me."

"Just because you've gotten used to it doesn't make it okay. Trust me... that wasn't normal. How she touched you. No."

He kissed her all over her face. "I'm sorry she scared you, Mel."

"Nothing that some good coffee and pancakes can't fix. Come on. I'm going to feed us."

He grinned, drawing him to her. "Not quite yet."

Well… sex could probably draw away the ghosts, too

* * *

THE DOORBELL RANG a second after an image of Lawson arriving on the property shot into the study. "It's Lawson," she let Elliot and Edward know. Edward was helping her go through one of the bigger boxes while Elliot wrote with headphones in his ears. Now that he was officially outed as the Bomber, he seemed to be pretty content spending all his time writing.

She was glad to see Lawson. Not only did she need an update on Peter Evans before she forgot the outside world existed, but she needed him to get her some things to study on ghosts.

"I'll go talk to him." She set down the file she was studying that listed all of the cows sold during the year and went out to go see the Enforcer. Elliot jumped up, following behind her.

He grabbed her hand. "You're really not okay because of what happened last night, are you?"

She sighed. "No. But I intend to rid the house of that ghost, and then I'll be better."

"I don't know if that's possible."

She stopped before she opened the door. "Anything is possible if I set my mind to it."

"Fair enough," he squeezed her fingers.

Lawson entered with his usual no nonsense stride. She didn't miss him glancing at their linked hands, but she doubted he'd mention it. "How are you guys?"

She cleared her throat. "We have a ghost problem."

He opened and closed his mouth. "I can't say that anyone has ever uttered those words to me before."

"Well, there's a first time for everything." Elliot rocked back on his heels. "Want a drink?"

Lawson looked between them. "I'll have a drink. That sounds great."

It did. With her mouth open, Melanie watched the two of them heading toward the kitchen. Lawson didn't usually stop and have a drink. Did he? She followed behind them as Elliot proceeded to spell the wine in the fridge to pour Lawson a glass. He helped himself to one, and the next thing she knew a glass appeared in her hand, too.

"Thanks." Lawson took a sip. "I'm officially off for the day. Long one. Peter is not easy to catch. At this point, I'd settle for catching him for doing something stupid like using magic in the human world. I could make him vanish for that. He's acting like the patron saint of good behavior right now."

Elliot nodded. "I knew him. Not knew him knew him, but I'd see him around. He's a scumbag. I used to feel like he wanted to hurt all the women in the room, like he watched them for the sake of figuring out how he could cause them harm. I couldn't concretely tell you why. Just that was what it used to feel like."

"Oh, he sets off all my creep alarms and then some. I always say when it comes to magic, trust your gut. Half of what I do and why I've been successful at it is that I listen to myself." He took another sip. "Ghosts? Really?"

"They've always been here. The question is really why Melanie never noticed them as a child." Elliot floated up to the counter and sat down on it. "She wants to get rid of them."

Lawson shook his head. "I'll see if I can dig anything up. Actually, I'll put Stefan on it. He is always into the obscure. Much more of a human legend than a magical one. Then again, Eleanor got possessed most of her life by an ancient witch. We do the weird in this friendship group pretty well. We'll miss you tonight."

She sipped her wine. "Is tonight one of Ava's dinners?"

"It is."

She leaned against the counter. "I'll miss you guys, too." The drink suddenly made more sense. Lawson did hate entertaining. It was just one of those things he did because his wife loved it. She was sure Lawson liked all of them, and it was clear he'd do anything for them considering the measures he was taking for her. But maybe the constant rotation of people eating at his house wasn't his favorite thing in the world.

He just loved Ava so much he put up with it.

"But you'll have an even number of people at the table for once," she grinned.

Lawson scowled at her. "You know no one cares about that. And you are bound to meet someone someday, Melanie. If you don't scare them off."

"No one who was worth it would ever be scared off by her." More wine poured into Elliot's glass. "I doubt you'd want someone like that hanging around anyway."

Lawson stared at Elliot. What was he assessing? It was almost like... No, there was no reason Lawson would be testing Elliot for anything.

"Nope," Lawson agreed. "I wouldn't. I never thought I'd be friends with Mitchell Sharpe, but he grew on me after he found Eleanor. I don't mind the dinner party people. They're my friends now, too. Family really. I wouldn't want Melanie with someone who got intimidated by how smart she was."

"That's nice, boys. Thanks for talking about me like I'm not here." She patted Lawson on the arm. "When I want you to big brother me I'll let you know. I'm pretty sure I'm several months older than you anyway."

He smirked. "Got it."

"Have the dinner party here." Elliot clapped his hands together. "Melanie can go if it's here. Why not just move the whole thing here tonight?"

She stared at him for a second waiting for the punchline. "You're kidding."

"No, why would I be? The house is great for entertaining. We'll do that. Here. Lawson, you can bring people in and out right? Safely? Your friends are not going to report Mel's location to Peter. Do it here."

She held up her hands. "Elliot, I don't cook. I mean, other than the making do we're doing. I can't host anyone here in your house."

"No, Ava would cook." Lawson set down his drink. "This sounds like a great idea. I'll go check with her, but assuming she doesn't say no, let's go with that."

Well, color her not surprised. Lawson was going to not have to have everyone in his own house for a change. She'd bet he'd be thrilled. "Elliot, I was going to talk to you about this. Who is cleaning the house? No one is ever here. I'm not sure we can get it ready in time. I'm happy to do my part but this place is huge. I'd want days to get it guest ready."

She did have strong feelings about the house being clean. It had been her mother's pride and joy for years.

"I am." He shrugged. "I have it on a constant spell to keep the floors we use clean. So not the attic or the basement but the rest of it."

That was a ton of magic. She shook her head. It wasn't her place to comment on how much energy he used up on a cleaning spell, even if she'd never have attempted that herself.

"All right, I guess if Elliot wants to have a dinner party… we'll have a dinner party."

His smile was huge. "Great."

CHAPTER 9

The house had alerted them to the fact that their company was arriving. Melanie stared at herself in the mirror. Well, Elliot's company. These were her friends, but it was his home. He'd invited them and there was no doubt in her mind he was doing it to be kind to her. She'd been off the whole day, thinking about ghosts. He probably wanted her to get happy again, to be a better houseguest. She couldn't blame him. This was exactly what she'd meant when she'd told him that she was just too much.

Melanie could never keep things easy.

But now her friends were here—well her married friends —and she was going to sit down and have dinner with all of them. Ava's food had arrived magically an hour before, and it had been cooking ever since. The house smelled delicious, like pot roast, potatoes, and asparagus. The wafting of the scent hit Mel hard and for a second, took her back in time, the way only a sense memory could.

She'd been told to wait on the bench in the front hall while her mother got something ready for a dinner party Elliot's mother had been having. Mrs. Boothe had come down the stairs wearing a long black dress and a string of pearls that had caught her attention. It was hard not to give Elliot's mother attention. She was beautiful, and also kind. The smell hadn't been pot roast. No, it had been something with garlic, but everything that was cooked in the kitchen at the main house always smelled like heaven to her.

Melanie blinked back to herself and the present. Elliot's mother was gone, following her husband to death, dying from a broken heart in the way that sometimes happened to those who were soul bound. But the house was still here. Elliot was still here. And Melanie did not in any way look like the lady of the house. She shook her head. She wasn't, never would be. This was a favor her friend was doing for her.

Some of her clothes had arrived, thanks to Lawson, and she was dressed in black pants, a black scoop neck top, and a gray blazer. She'd managed to style it up just a little bit with a black belt that had a silver ring around it. Her black canvas sneakers completed whatever this look was that she was going for.

Melanie spent most of her time in dark suits for court, gray suits for the office, and her yoga pants when she was home. She'd tried to dress up and that was ridiculous because Elliot didn't have the slightest idea what she wore.

He looked sexy as hell. For a man who couldn't see to dress himself, he certainly knew his clothing well enough to pull out an outfit he could have worn to any of the top restaurants in town and ended up in a magazine. He wore jeans and a plaid, tailored to fit him, collared shirt beneath a black blazer. The blue and pink in his shirt would have once brought out his blue eyes. Now, he covered his eyes with his dark glasses and still managed to not look ridiculous.

Elliot really was the best looking man she'd ever seen anywhere.

"Hey…" Eleanor caught her attention. When had they actually gotten inside? Wow, she was distracted. "You look so pretty. Did you put on makeup?"

She had, which was really pathetic. "Eleanor, I'm… not making good choices. Come on, let's go have dinner."

"He's cute. I had no idea because I've never seen him before, but when he let us in, I thought oh wow, good job, Melanie. Unless you don't think so."

She linked their arms. "I've always felt that way. But it's an impossibility, and I'm being a stupid girl."

"I was a stupid girl, once. And he's in the other room right now laughing at something Elliot is saying. Sometimes it's not stupid… sometimes it's gutsy."

She knew that Eleanor was right but circumstances were different. "He's got a curse they can't get off, and it's going to kill him like it has every male in his family for generations."

"Yes." Eleanor squeezed her. "Let's hope for the best. I was taken over by an ancient witch. They cured me. Maybe it's not too late yet. Besides, he must really like you to do this. I mean, who wants to have six people over for dinner that you don't know from a hole in the wall while you're battling a curse?"

That was true. "He's very sweet."

And talented. Smart. Kind. Funny. She could go on and on. Yep, she had it bad. Stupid girl.

The dining room buzzed with conversation. Elliot stood in the center of it all wearing his sunglasses and laughing at something that Stefan said. That was unusual. Stefan was dry, not usually funny. But they were laughing at something just the same. He turned when she entered and put out his hand.

He couldn't see her and yet he knew when she'd shown up in a room full of conversation. She linked her fingers with his. "Nice to see you all," she spoke to the room. "Thanks for coming. I haven't seen all of you since the night I got myself into this mess."

"If you want to be technical, you got yourself into this mess when you took her as a client." Lawson shrugged. "Semantics, I suppose."

"Yep, I screwed this one. Sorry for that. I can't imagine what that would have been like to have to be there and see me go down like that, knowing..."

Elliot shook his head, interrupting her. "You're not apologizing for getting attacked and hurt, right? I assure you whatever their discomfort was it didn't touch yours."

Ava nodded. "True. Dinner is ready. And I think I've figured out the lay of the land here so let's all eat. Thanks for this, Elliot. It's good to see my bestie again. I've been worried sick."

After that, the conversation was easy. She'd never had a partner to sit with at one of these dinners before. Elliot was clearly practiced at this kind of interaction. He talked easily with one person and then another, the whole time keeping his hand on her knee. Did he know that she sometimes got nervous in crowds even though these were her friends? Or that she loved going out but still preferred quite a bit to stay home and that problem was why meeting people was so hard?

Maybe he just wanted her again so he kept his hand on her knee. Whatever the reason, it helped.

"You have a huge amount of power." Stefan spoke to Elliot but informed the room. "Part of what I can do is almost... taste the power of those around me. I think you're more powerful than me. That's unusual."

Elliot shrugged. "Power only matters in regards to what you do with it. A person could have a ton and do little with it."

That was true, except that he composed in his sleep, and

his magic let him do it. He was apparently running a constant cleaning spell and who knew what else he was doing behind the scenes.

Stefan shook his head. "No. You're not a small user. I can feel that, too."

Kim touched the back of his neck. "Now, honey, we talked about how it's not polite to talk about people's power usage."

Stefan sighed. "Sorry. I sometimes forget my manners."

"It's all right." Elliot sighed. "You're right, of course. I use a ton of power. I've always had a lot of it and used it as I saw fit."

"It's amazing that they didn't tap you to be an Enforcer." Kim looked between everyone. "That kind of power range is usually a shoo-in to the Enforcer program. They come at us hard."

Elliot shrugged. "I'm cursed. From the moment I was born everyone knew that would be the case. I wasn't exactly Enforcer material, I don't think." He waved his hand. "I've kept busy. I don't think I could do what you guys do. Even with everything happening, I'm pretty much an optimist. It would kill me to have seen nothing but the dregs of the witching world in my grown up years while I was able to see."

Stefan lifted his drink. "You're right about that."

Things eased after that. Lots of laughter, and the food was fantastic. Ava had always been a great cook but after her powers opened up and she could literally hear the Earth talking to her, she'd gotten even better at it.

"Elliot." Lawson sighed. "You have to tell me the truth, brother. It isn't the house with the security spell, is it? It's you. You've somehow spelled the house, and you're keeping it constantly on."

Melanie's mouth fell open. Between that and the cleaning,

a healthy witch would be constantly wrecked. How was Elliot doing this and dealing with the curse, too?"

He set down his drink. "Guilty."

"Can you teach me how? I have hidden my home away pretty well, but I don't have this."

Elliot winced. "Maybe a year ago." He pulled off his glasses. "I'm afraid I'm pretty far into this nastiness now. I don't know that I can really teach anyone magic anymore."

Lawson stared at Elliot for a long moment. "That sucks."

"Yes." His smile was wry. "It does."

"You could be so bitter," Kim's voice was low. "Yet you're not. You're cheerful. You're helping Melanie."

Stefan nodded. "He was the king of all sports back in school. We used to watch him in awe."

"That was then. I'm not exactly the same now. Even when I could see. But I had a choice in life. My old man leveled with me early on. I could be angry or I could say that I'd enjoy every day I was here and leave it at that. So I chose the latter. It's been easier." He squeezed her knee. "Mostly."

Ava sat forward. "It's like the Bomber play. Funny how those always resonate with me. Sometimes we have to listen to our parents even when it's hard. They have good advice, even if they're not always good people."

"I really thought the point of that was that the son himself was not such a golden child." Mitchell shrugged. "I think it works on both levels."

Lawson took a sip of his drink. "Makes you wonder about Bomber himself, right? What has he or she been through?"

Melanie stared at Lawson. Did he know? It was always hard to tell with the Enforcer. He could very well be aware of Elliot's secret identity. But... maybe not. "Do you think that it matters? I mean he could be a rich guy living in a mansion or a poor woman trying to put food on the table for her kids. What does it matter if it makes you feel something?"

"I'm never going to seek out the identity. Everyone deserves privacy as long as they're not breaking the laws."

Elliot sat back in his seat. "Everyone got enough to drink?"

"Have you seen the Bomber plays?" Eleanor asked Elliot with a sweet tone.

"Not lately." He waved his hand and another round poured into the drinks.

"Oh." Mitchell sat up. "I translated the notebook you sent me, Mel. It was very old spells. Seriously, Almaric descent. I don't know if they even work. I don't mess with the ancient spells anymore. But it's something to do with wealth and sacrifice. Whoever tried those was a sick fuck." He laughed. "To put it not gently."

Elliot shook his head. "Sorry, I've missed something. What are we talking about?"

"The notebook I sent Mitchell. He translated it." She put out her hand, and Mitchell floated it to her. She stared down at it. This told her very little. Someone had saved a book of weird spells about money? The Boothes had plenty, and it had nothing to do with their curse. Or did it? She chewed on her bottom lip as another thought occurred to her. "Mitchell, we have a ghost problem in this house. Can you help? Or you, Stefan?"

Stefan nodded. "Lawson messaged me about that."

"A ghost problem?" Mitchell looked between them. "Really? Isn't that like a human fear or something? Like they don't have enough things to worry about so let's make the house haunted in our imaginations?"

She pointed at him. "Think about your wife for a second..."

He held up his hand. "Got it. I'll look into ghosts."

Eleanor smiled. "I will, too. I'm good at the unusual. It's

more my specialty than his these days. Can we see the ghosts?"

"Maybe." As if on cue, the noise in the attic sounded and everyone but Elliot looked up. "That's one. But we can never find it. Faceless."

Stefan jumped to his feet. "Like hell. If there is something to find, I find it."

He shot upward into the air and Kim groaned. "Here we go. He'll be in that attic the rest of the night."

Elliot took Melanie's hand. "Remind me, what this journal is? I'm... I don't remember."

"Oh, we talked about it. Sorry, maybe you were distracted. I found a journal I couldn't read and asked if I could send it to Mitchell. You said yes."

He rubbed his eyes. "I'm getting a headache."

"Let's send everyone home." She got to her feet. "Ava, I think we need to send you guys on with dessert."

Her friend nodded, understanding shining in her eyes. "I'm going to send over another drink tomorrow for him."

"That would be great." Melanie strode to the other side of the table to hug her friend. Ava had a big heart. She would worry all night. Of course, Mel was probably going to be up doing the same.

Kim sighed and pointed toward the ceiling, sending a talking spell upwards as she spoke. "Stefan, we're leaving. Or I am with your unborn child. If you want to stay here and ghost hunt, that's your own business."

He popped right next to her. "I couldn't find a thing. Mel, I'll send you whatever I have on ghosts. As Mitchell said, it's human folklore. But we'll see what we can do."

Mitchell walked over. "Yes, whatever Ellie and I can find, we'll send."

"Thanks."

Lawson tugged his wife next to him. "And in the meantime, I'm catching Peter. This week. I can feel it in my gut."

She turned to Elliot who was doing his best to say goodnight to everyone and not bring attention to his headache. He'd put his sunglasses back on. She doubted that did anything, but maybe it just made him feel better. Her friends exited quickly.

Elliot turned toward her. "Mel, you here?"

Well, that was a change. He usually seemed to be able to sense her. "I am. Hey, why don't you head up to bed? I'll clean up here. And no, don't you dare use your magic for this tonight. I'm going to do it."

He sighed, his smile forming back on his face. "Going to bed isn't going to fix this headache tonight. I doubt I will sleep. But yes, I'll let you clean. I do feel wiped. Just not used to so many people, I guess. That sucks. I used to be social. I'll sit here and let you spell away the mess like some kind of loser who doesn't help."

Elliot sat, and she ran a hand through his hair. "You are so not that."

It took her ten minutes to spell cast the whole area clean, plus she had to send Ava all of her cooking supplies back to the safe address that Lawson had them using. By the time she got finished, Elliot had his head in his hands.

"Come on. Let's go rest." She nudged him, and he lifted his head, pulling his glasses off.

This was one of those few times she could actually tell he was sad. He rose, and she wrapped her arms around his waist. He spoke when they were about halfway to his bedroom. "I forgot something tonight. That notebook. I still can't remember what you told me was in it… I'm even sort of forgetting you told me. That's not a good sign, Mel."

Her heart clenched. "That's a small thing."

"Small things first. Details go. Then bigger things. Eventually, it all goes until there is nothing but raving lunacy."

She'd seen it up to the last part. His mother had shut down the house when his father reached the final stages. "It's still early days."

"No, it's not." He shook his head, following her into the bedroom. "Edward has specific instructions about what to do with me when this all goes askew. I don't want you near me when I'm gone. When I'm just a shell, okay? I want your promise on that."

It was hard to imagine him like that. "Okay." She hated making that promise, but everyone was entitled to say how they wanted things to go at the end. "How's your head?"

He put his hand on his forehead. "Awful."

"I'm sorry about that." She looked away. "I've gone and done something really stupid. I think you should know because I have to take steps to protect myself."

He tilted his head to the side. "What do you mean?"

"I went and fell for you. Or maybe I... oh forget the maybe... I harbored old feelings. It doesn't really matter. You were clear on things, and I've gone and screwed it up. So I am going to try to pull back a little from this before I topple head over heels and you have to throw me out of the house for being so ridiculous."

He opened and closed his mouth. "That was brave, what you just said. You could have kept that to yourself or just distanced yourself and I'd never have known why."

It might have been brave but now all she wanted to do was get out of the room. "Well, honesty really is the best policy. Keeps things simpler. I'll leave you to your night. I think for my own heart I just have to..."

"Mel, wait." He stepped toward her. "My turn to be honest."

She swallowed. "If you're just going to tell me you warned

me, that you were clear, that all the obvious things were stated blatantly, I am already doing that in my own head. As I told Eleanor tonight, I'm a stupid girl."

"You're not." He took another step toward her. "You spoke truth. So will I." He took a long breath. "Of course I knew you had fallen for me. To not know, would be to seek denial and I'm not doing that. Just the way you have to know that my feelings for you have gone beyond friendship. I could to that thing people do and pretend otherwise. I could be a liar. But I'm not. What I am is selfish, and I've lost all integrity because I'm going to ask you not to do what you want to do, which is to take yourself emotionally away from me. I wouldn't blame you if you did. Only, I'm going to ask you not to do that, Mel."

The conversation had not gone as she'd anticipated. "Elliot, we've hardly known each other. How I feel about you, it's not okay. I was a child the last time you saw me and now here we are, you suffering and blind. I came into your home. I'm here. I'm someone to…"

"No. You think just anyone could have inspired me to want to somehow live again? It's you, Melanie. The second you walked in to help me that day I knew that I wanted you. I'm so fucked for even thinking it. I don't get to want anything, right. I'm nearing the end stage of this curse. But I'm going to ask you to not do what you should do because I'm a selfish bastard."

Tears leaked from her eyes, and he strode all the way to her, wiping them away. "Elliot…"

"No, go." He stepped back. "I'm not going to emotionally blackmail you. I care about you, too. If I was allowed to think of a future, I'd put you in it. But I'm not. So you need to get away from me before we're both just ridiculous. In fact, you should call Lawson and get him to move you some-place else. Surely there has to be a place you'd be more comfortable than watching me become a shell of myself. Go. Please."

He turned his back on her. She didn't move for a second, but then she made her feet cooperate. Melanie didn't have the wherewithal to float away. She had to do it the old-fashioned way. Forcing herself to take the steps in what could only be called scurrying, she made it to the room she'd claimed as hers.

Methodically, she stripped off her clothes, put on her ugliest pajamas, walked to the bathroom to wash her face, and then went back into the room to climb into bed. She didn't shed any tears. Instead, it was like she couldn't turn off her mind.

He cared about her, too, and he was sending her away so she wouldn't get more hurt. Melanie covered her eyes with her arm, but sleep didn't come. She rolled the length of the bed and then back again before giving up on that. He cared about her. Why did it keep coming back to that?

Finally, she had enough. She wasn't going to be Peter Evans's wife. No one was ever going to look at her and say she didn't know what she was doing.

On bare feet, she stomped back through the house to Elliot's room. The sound of low playing music greeted her as she came through the door. If he was sleeping, she'd leave him alone. Instead, what she found was Elliot lying across the bed on his stomach. She didn't know what this music was, but it seemed to be just strings, no words or other music accompanying it.

He looked up when she entered. "Mel?"

"It's me."

Elliot got up on his knees. "I... I'm sorry if I've already caused you pain."

"You've rescued me. Saved me. Given me more joy than I have the right to want. In a time when I should be nothing but miserable." Melanie walked toward him fast, taking his hands in hers. "But I want us both to do this knowing what we're doing and not pretending otherwise. I am choosing to continue down this road, knowing it will lead me to pain. I want it anyway."

He flared his nostrils. "No, I don't want that for you."

She wrapped her arms around his neck. "Then it's a good thing you don't get to tell me what to do."

He ran his hands down her arms. "Fuck."

"Yes, in a second."

He groaned at her bad joke. "Melanie, come on. This ends when I'm raving and gone to madness. You'll leave, and then you'll be in nothing but pain. You'll wish we hadn't done this tonight."

She kissed him, his soft mouth meeting hers. Elliot sighed against her lips, the fight leaving his muscles. When she spoke, it was in a whisper. "I'll regret the things I didn't do more than the future pain I'm consenting to have. Kiss me again."

He did.

She shut her eyes for a second just to feel the closeness before she opened them again. This time, she pushed him backward until she could climb on top of him on the bed. He smiled up at her. Melanie's heart swelled. There were no untruths between them now. She might someday hate her heartache but right then she was just glad to have this time.

CHAPTER 10

*M*elanie kissed him until her head swam. He made a rough sound in his throat before he peeled her shirt off of her. They hadn't discussed it, but the way things had gone, it did seem like the kind of night to use their hands and not their spells. She did the same for him, pulling his trendy collared shirt over his head and discarding it to the floor.

He pressed his forehead onto her shoulder, and she kissed his cheek. "It's okay to tell me your head hurts too much for this."

"It's fine." He met her gaze, his white unseeing eyes and her own holding for a second, like they could really see each other. "I was just wishing I could have seen what you were wearing tonight. I should have asked. You spent a lot of time getting ready."

She smiled and touched the side of his face, the way he did with her, stroking her thumb across the shape of his nose. There was the slightest bump there. He must have broken it and not seen a healer at some point. The slight imperfection did nothing to detract from how utterly beautiful he was.

"What were you wearing?" he asked again.

"Black and gray, basically. Coat was gray. The rest of me was black. Very simple. I have few things that aren't work clothes."

He nodded. "Sounds pretty. With your dark hair, I bet it was."

She ran her hands over his strong abs, tracing each one of them. There was no hurrying tonight. She wondered if he felt that, too.

He stroked his hand from her chin, down her neck, to her chest. She shivered, goosebumps breaking out on her skin. Yes, she wanted him. He tilted his head to the side. "You smell like strawberries. I love it."

She did? "I've been using whatever soap and shampoo you have here. I'm not sure what it smells like other than clean."

He grinned. "No, it's your natural scent." He placed his nose up against her skin, breathing her in deeply.

Elliot kissed her, from her chin down to her stomach. She shuddered. This was... heaven, as the humans would say. He tugged off her pants and then her underwear, throwing them aside.

"You still have your clothes on, and I can't reach them."

He laughed, before he spelled them away. She groaned. "I liked taking them off you."

"Next time. Besides, I'm so hard it would have hurt." He smiled at her. "You do that to me."

She kissed his chin. "If you say so."

"I do. And proof, as they say, is in the visualization of it, right? Take a look, baby."

He'd never called her that before, and she liked the endearment as much as she did enjoy the size of his cock.

She reached forward and stroked it. He sucked in his breath. "Damn."

"I know I'm supposed to just look with my eyes. But how could I resist touching it if you're going to point it out like that?"

She loved when Elliot gave her what she thought of as his sardonic grin. "Do I seem like I'm complaining, Mel?"

No, he really didn't.

He dropped his head, which made it impossible for her to keep her grip on his cock because of the reshuffling of their bodies. His head was back where it was before. Elliot kissed both of her thighs before planting a kiss on her pussy. She cried out just from the smooth feel of his lips on her most sensitive spot.

He licked his tongue over her clit, really seeming to focus his attention there. She closed her eyes, enjoying the moment and not letting herself think of anything else. He grabbed onto one of her knees and squeezed. It helped. He must have remembered what oral was like for her. She needed him to keep her here, or she'd oh… He squeezed her knee again.

Elliot lifted his head; his nostrils flared. "I want to do this all night, but I need you so much, baby. Can I… can I make it up to you?"

Make it up to her? Did he think she was upset? "Elliot, I need you too and there is nothing I'd like more than you inside of me."

He nodded. "Thank fuck for that."

She grinned at his phrasing as he pushed himself inside of her. Her body stretched to meet him. The few times they'd been together now had gotten her better at accommodating him when he first pressed his cock deep inside of her. She loved the feeling.

Melanie wrapped her arms around his neck and held on. This time was different. His movements were less practiced.

He was really lost to this and that was just what she wanted because she was, too. He jerked against her clit, and she shattered. There had been so much tension it was like she simply needed to… explode.

Her back arched, pushing her sensitive nipples into his chest. He moaned a long sound before he emptied inside of her. She panted, barely able to breathe but never happier in her whole life.

Whatever might go wrong could go wrong later.

For now, there was just bliss.

* * *

IF THE GHOST came during the night, Melanie didn't notice. It was possible that Elliot knew. He hadn't slept, not a wink. He hadn't even seemed all that surprised about it, and they'd gone down to breakfast like he'd had a good night's sleep.

Three books plus a shake from Ava greeted her in the kitchen. Mitchell, Stefan, and Eleanor had all sent ghost books. In addition to finally getting through the rest of the boxes, she at least knew what she was going to be doing that day.

Elliot yawned, his only indication so far of being tired, before he sat down to drink coffee and ate in silence. He looked up and grinned at her. "You're quiet."

"I'm thinking about going through these books."

He nodded. "You read. I'll write."

She loved how he didn't need entertainment because he could simply find something to take away his attention any time he wanted. Maybe someone else would want to be constantly talked to, but she'd never been that person.

Melanie sat down to read.

Ten minutes later she was taking notes. Usually, she did this just for cases, to go over the law. Witching laws were complicated. They were derived from human laws from the times witches had been in hiding, but ultimately, they were more complicated. She was good at picking them apart. Melanie didn't have a lot of clients these days, but the ones she had usually won.

She sighed. Unless, they were murdered by their ex-husbands. Melanie set that aside. There was nothing—yet—she could do about Peter Evans, but she would. She'd find a way. If she could ever dig him out of the shallow grave Lawson might put him in.

She started reading. The journal that Mitchell translated, that Elliot couldn't keep a memory of, was odd. These weren't spells she'd ever seen anywhere, and she had been in ancient and advanced spell casting in school. Still, it was strange.

Spells were about moving pieces of magic that already existed through the filter of a witch's own personal skills, the things they could naturally do. It was a mixture of instinct, natural ability, and training. She'd always been pretty high up in power, but she'd never be able to do certain things because she didn't have the natural affinity for it. No one knew what they had until the powers manifested sometime in adolescence or maybe slightly later.

And these spells seemed… off. It was like it was trying to create magic where there wasn't any magic to begin with.

She chewed on her lip and tapped the table.

"Reading something interesting?" Elliot plopped down next to her as Edward came into the room carrying a box that he started loading dishes into. She watched him for a second before she answered Elliot.

"Why would your ancestor have needed spells to create magic?"

He scratched his head. "Who?"

She held up the journal. Not that he could see it. "The

journal you're having trouble remembering, it's about creating magic."

His face fell. "I'm forgetting things. When did that happen?"

Edward stopped packing the box with the good china and stared at them. She made eye contact with the man before she placed her hand on Elliot's shoulder. "Don't worry about it. Seriously. Not important." She kissed his cheek. The last thing she wanted to do was make him upset. "I'm just studying something, and I'm about to set it down and see if I can get rid of the ghosts here because it seems nonsensical to me."

He groaned. "Mel, I've told you that they've always been here."

"Yes, but why don't I know about them?"

The house groaned and a second later the doorbell rang. A picture popped above the table, and Melanie sat forward.

Elliot chewed his fingernail. "It has to be an Enforcer to get through the wards. Who is it?"

"Lawson, and he has my parents with him." She was on her feet. Melanie hadn't seen her parents since the night she'd almost died. How long had that been? Days? She was losing track of things in this house.

"Your parents? Awesome." Elliot got to his feet as she rushed to greet them at the door.

She missed them so much that she didn't let them say a word before her arms were around them, squeezing them both tightly. Mel didn't see them very much on a day-to-day basis, but right then she'd never been so happy to see her family as she was in that moment.

Lawson nodded at her. "They wanted to see you. I'll be back in a few hours. We may finally have him, Mel. He's getting sloppy. Thinks we've moved on."

She grinned at him. "Thanks."

"No problem. Thanks for last night, Elliot."

They shook hands, and whatever they said to each other, she ignored because her mother cupped her cheeks in her hands. "You look so much better than the last time I saw you."

"I feel so much better."

Her father looked around. "It's so strange to be here. Looks like we never left."

A pop indicated Lawson had left, and Elliot turned toward her father who embraced him. The move startled her before she remembered the simple fact that they'd known him when he'd been a young child and had watched him grow up. Elliot thought of them as family in a world where he had none. Her mother let go of her and hugged him longer than her father had.

"Welcome. So glad to ah… see you." He smirked. "So to speak."

"Oh, Elliot." Her mother sniffed. "It was one thing to see it over the messaging, another to see you like this. I'm so sorry."

He shrugged. "You know us Boothe men, we have to make big exits. Come in, are you hungry?"

She smiled. "His mother was like that. She'd offer me food when I showed up for work every day while my own home—on her own property, that she kept stocked with food that she'd paid for—was a hundred yards away from her front door."

He grinned, looking over his shoulder. "I'd forgotten that. Thanks for that memory."

She lost her own smile. Memory. His was going. Now he didn't even know he'd forgotten the journal. She rubbed the back of her neck and tried not to dwell on it. This was a natural progression of something she couldn't control.

Melanie looked down at her feet. She had to pull this together. Her parents would see right through it.

He spun around. "Hey, here's a question. You guys saw the ghosts when you lived here?"

"Oh yes, I actually learned some gardening techniques from the one outside. Sure, that crew has always been here. How many were there? Five?" Her father nodded as he spoke.

Her mother held up her fingers. "Six."

With a rub of his chin, Elliot spoke again. "So tell me how it is that you know all that, and that Melanie was here all the time as a child, but she has never seen the ghosts before now?"

Her parents were quiet. They looked at each other and then back at him. Elliot tilted his head to the side. "Mel, am I missing non-verbal communication?"

She stepped toward him, taking his hand. Doing so in front of her parents should have felt weird but it didn't. Maybe she was just too far down this path to care. "You are. What's going on, Mom and Dad?"

"Melanie, we lived and worked here. Mrs. Boothe was a caring employer. Mr. Boothe took a real interest in you. And you... were terrified of those ghosts to the point that you wouldn't come in the house. At the age of five you downright refused. It was terrible. We couldn't leave you, and you weren't quite in school yet. Mrs. Boothe offered to get a nanny for us, but we were not going to let her do that."

Elliot scrunched up his nose. "I don't remember this at all."

"Well, you were a teenager. I doubt very much that you were focusing on the running of the house." Her mother laughed, waving her hand in the air. "We had to do something."

Melanie knew the answer. "You spelled it away. I couldn't see them. I became blind to ghosts."

Her mother winced. "Not the most wonderful parenting technique, I'll grant you. But it worked. You couldn't see them, and we told you they were gone. I think if you don't remember that, then you've simply forgotten. You were very young."

"And to be fair," her father interjected. "We made it so the spell fell away when you were eighteen."

She chewed on her lips. "I haven't been back here since then."

It was not a great feeling to know that she'd had a spell on her for thirteen years that had altered reality for her. Parents doing this to their children were a little bit... not spoken of. It was a dirty little secret that no one discussed. If the child had an unreasonable fear that was somehow affecting life in a negative way, they could make that stop. Healers wouldn't participate, but they didn't get in the way of it.

Melanie had never imagined it could happen to her.

Elliot stroked a finger over her hand. "Hold still, Mel."

A warmth traveled up her arm, and he tilted his head in the way that he did when he was thinking about things. His smile was fast. "You don't have any other spells on you that are affecting your mind at all. You're clear."

"You can tell that?" She shouldn't have doubted it considering Kim could have seen it, too, but it was never bad to be reassured.

He nodded. "Yep."

Her mother patted him on the arm. "He always was incredibly powerful. His father was too, but it's like it doubled in him."

That was interesting. Elliot was incredibly strong. Just not enough to ward off a curse that the best healers in existence could do nothing for him. Not enough to save his mind. She blinked away her tears.

"Coffee?" Melanie asked her parents. She'd never in all her years heard her father say no to caffeine. He didn't this time either.

127

* * *

SEVERAL HOURS LATER, the house alerted them that Lawson was back, and her parents rose to their feet to leave. It had been such a nice, easy visit, but she needed to get back to studying the books she'd been sent if she was going to make sense of this at all.

Her father stopped to shake Elliot's hand, and her mother linked her arm with Melanie's.

"So," the older woman whispered. "You and Elliot?"

Her cheeks heated up. They'd done nothing to hide it and her parents were smart, intuitive people. "We both know this can't go anywhere. For now, it just feels right."

Her mother cupped Mel's cheek. "There will be nothing but pain with this. You're a grown woman, and if things were different and Elliot wasn't... going to end the way he was... I'd be thrilled. He's the first person I've ever seen you have chemistry with. And he made you laugh a lot today. I just worry. Come home when this is over, and we'll figure out your next step together. It can't be all or nothing, Mel."

She didn't understand that last part. "What do you mean?"

"You had to leave the big corporate magical law firms because they stifled you. I get that. You always worked best alone. But then you went straight into being you versus the bad witches out there all alone." She sighed. "Isn't there some sort of safe in between?"

That was a good question. "I don't know. I need to figure that all out. I'll come see you when this is over. After I get rid of the ghosts."

"Easier to get rid of the ghosts than think about other things?" Her mother cocked her eyebrow and Melanie resisted groaning. No matter how old she got there were still things her mother did that made her feel like she was five.

Not to mention she was probably right. Her parents left

quickly after that, leaving her with Elliot, alone in the hall. Edward had said he was going to make sure they had everything they needed for the gardeners—the living kind—to come next week. She hadn't seen him in a while.

She turned toward Elliot. "It was good to see them."

"For me, too. Your dad is so funny. I forgot about his wicked sense of humor. What were we doing right before they got here?"

Had he forgotten because it was another thing he'd lost or just in the course of things that happened sometimes?

"I was going to study up on ghosts." She deliberately didn't tell him about the journal. Not remembering it made him stressed, and she didn't want to do that to him. Anxiety couldn't help anything.

"Oh, that's right." His smile told her this wasn't a lost memory. "And I'm going to write. Let's do that. Then I want to get you naked again."

Her cheeks immediately heated up. "Does it bother you that my parents totally know we're sleeping together?"

His mouth fell open. "Do they?"

"They do." Had he not picked up on that? "It was probably the holding hands."

He scratched his head. "You told your parents we were holding hands?"

"No, they just saw it. When they were here." As she spoke the words she realized what was happening. Her heart fell into her stomach.

"When were your parents here?" Elliot paled.

So this was going to be how it happened. It wasn't only that he'd forget the journal. That was a small thing. Who cared anyway? Elliot didn't remember that her parents had just left. Her body went cold for a second. She rubbed her arms.

"Come on, let's go get something done today."

He rubbed his eyes. "Did I forget something?"

Was it better to tell him or not tell him? He'd completely forgotten that he forgot the journal. Maybe it didn't matter at all. There wasn't any making a memory for this.

"No." She took his hand. "Let's go. You're going to write, and I'm going to work."

"Sounds like a plan."

She leaned her head on his arm as they floated together toward the study. She'd only had him for such a short period of time, and she was going to lose him memory-by-memory, moment-by-moment. Curses were always insidious, and she fucking hated this one.

* * *

MELANIE STOOD IN THE YARD. It rained slightly on her, but no one would know what she was doing if she stayed out here. Besides, the weather matched her mood.

"Okay," she spoke aloud. Elliot was inside writing, as he'd been doing for hours, and the books she'd read hadn't told her much about how to get rid of ghosts. They were more like folklore. Things humans believed in to explain the unexplainable, when witches had working magic to make the unexpected happen.

But anything could be handled with the right kind of spell. Heck, her parents had made her ghost blind. That meant ... well, she wasn't sure what that meant, but it meant something.

A witch learned a spell and then didn't have to say the spell anymore because their body could simply perform it, like muscle memory. Repeat it enough and you could just do it. Some people—Lawson—could make up a spell in his head and never need to say it aloud. Elliot, too, for that matter.

For some things, that was true for Melanie. She didn't

have to learn a spell and teach it to herself to cook. That she could mostly figure out and just spell it instantly. But other things she'd had to work hard to learn to do.

The question was could she still learn things or had she become too set in her ways and unable to keep expanding.

If she was going to try to make sense of that journal, she had to figure it out. Thunder bellowed in the sky, and she sighed. No, she wasn't going to be afraid of this. Not today. There were assassins who wanted to kill her, storms in the sky, ghosts on the premises, and Elliot was forgetting things. All of these things could terrify her into non-movement except that she wasn't going to let them.

She wanted to learn the first spell in the journal. It had to do with controlling the flow of water. Outside of the Boothe house was a river. She used to walk up and down it when she was a girl, getting her feet and the bottom of her pants wet as she splashed. There were tadpoles turning into frogs, and she'd never been able to resist watching it happen, year after year.

Melanie walked there now. Learning a spell from a book was a skill she'd forgotten. Still, maybe if she just read it aloud, that would help.

She cleared her throat and set her shoulders. Melanie would do this until it worked, to reteach herself how to learn, and then she'd write a spell to rid the house of ghosts. That sounded as good a plan as any to not let herself cry over Elliot.

What would he forget next?

She shook her head. Couldn't think about that now. No, she had a project. She was going to do it.

"Water up, water down. Water, water, turn around." She read the words and then stared at the river. What in the hell was that? Melanie took a deep breath. Elliot's ancestor who'd written this book must have been an idiot.

It was like the kind of spell you would give a child. It rhymed. Adult spells were single words. Sometimes numbers and degrees, depending on what the practitioner wanted to do.

Why don't you play with me anymore, Melanie?

The sound made her turn around. Standing at the window of the house, staring down at her, was a little girl. Not just any girl but the occupant of the room Melanie was temporarily calling her own. The room Elliot said was creepy.

Melanie stared up at her. Fuck. She'd played with the ghost many times before her mother had made her ghost blind. She just hadn't known the little girl was dead.

Her breath caught in her throat. The gardener had rambled, been unaware. But the little girl—Elliot's dead ancestor—had called her Melanie.

What did that mean? Mel shut the journal. The strange water spell could wait. She was starting with her former playmate.

CHAPTER 11

She made her way upstairs and into the bedroom quickly. Her arms were wet, a result of being rained on, and she shivered as the cooler air inside hit her damp skin. Yes, she was going with that and not that she was terrified to do this.

Melanie could vaguely remember this ghost and how they'd played together. Her mother had thought it was cute and one day used the word ghost to describe it. That had been the end of it for Mel. How was it that at five she'd known it wasn't okay to hang around with ghosts but every other person in this space was so fine with it? She shook her head.

Whatever the reason, enough was enough.

"Melanie, why don't you play with me anymore?"

Mel steeled her spine. "I don't play with anyone anymore. I'm… an adult now."

The little girl was dark haired, pale, with big brown eyes. She would have been a beautiful child and probably not scary in life, as she was in death. The too pale skin and the big eyes made her creepy when living they would have made her stunning. Funny how that worked.

She put her hand on her hips. "Well, pooh. You've been ignoring me."

Melanie continued to stare at her. "I couldn't see you." Or hear her, apparently. She shook her head. How did the spell work? She'd have to look it up, later. Truth was she had enough spells going on to deal with that one. It was what it was, and she couldn't undo it. Nor would she want to. She'd been blissfully unaware of ghosts during her early years, and she wouldn't mind being blissfully unaware of them now.

Well… maybe not.

"How do you know me? How do you know things? The man outside… he doesn't."

She sat down on the floor. A doll appeared in her arms, and she rocked it slowly. "The man upstairs says I'm special because I'm family."

Melanie blinked. "The man upstairs? Who is that?"

They were never able to find anyone up there despite the noise. The girl lifted her eyebrows and threw her hair over her shoulder. "I want to play. Not talk."

That was too bad. Melanie really didn't know how to compel a ghost to speak. She hadn't seen anything about that in the books she'd been given. Humans sometimes used boards called Ouija to speak to them but the ghosts seemed happy to communicate. How did one force a ghost to talk?

For now, maybe she'd go along with this and hope that she got some kind of information she needed. If that didn't work, the only thing she'd lost was time.

Mel plopped down on the floor. "All right, what are we playing?"

For the next hour, she moved blocks using magic, talked to the dead girl's doll, and hid under the bed for the sake of keeping the ghost happy. They were children's games she'd once played, too. Particularly the moving of the blocks. It was a standard game for learning to control magic.

It was terrible even if it was surreal. "Why are you here?" She eventually had to ask the question. "I don't see ghosts other places. Ever. Just this house. Do you know? Is it some kind of magical portal or…"

The little girl—whose name she had learned was Hannah—leaned forward. "It's because the man upstairs, my grandfather, did something. And we are stuck. I don't want to be here. I want to go. Like my mama went, like my papa went. Like most everyone else goes. Like Elliot will go. Unless he gets stuck, too."

Melanie hated that idea on so many levels. First the idea that Elliot was going to go at all made her stomach clench and even worse was the idea he might be stuck in this house. All of it was just too terrible for words.

"Why can we never see the man upstairs? We hear him, but we can't see him?"

The little girl shrugged. "I guess you're blind."

Wait… she wasn't. She was going to ask Hannah what she meant, but the ghost vanished like she'd never been there, even her toys poofing away. Melanie sighed, rubbing away the goosebumps on her arms.

Okay, she'd gotten through that and had some information. There absolutely was a ghost in the attic. And somehow she was blind.

* * *

DAYS LATER, Melanie wasn't any closer to understanding anything than she'd been before. Lawson had been in touch and there was no movement. She chewed on her fingernail as she stared at the river. It had been raining every day, so hard that she hadn't wanted to risk going anywhere near the river to try her spells from the odd book.

Not to mention, Elliot's rapid paced memory loss made her want to never leave his side. But she wasn't going to reach her goals any quicker if she didn't start to do something about them.

"Tell me again what you're doing with the river?" Elliot came up behind her. "It's not a memory thing. I just don't get it."

She couldn't blame him on that. "I don't really know." She leaned back against him for a second to feel his body heat before she pulled herself forward. Concentration was the name of the game. "I just want to see what happens. This has something to do with the river, and it's in a book I found."

That was easier than the journal discussion. When he forgot something, it was best just to act like it didn't exist at all. So far that had been the journal, her parents' visit, spaghetti, and the color of his mother's hair. The last one seemed the trickiest because he would think about her often and stumble through that moment. It was hard for him to not remember something like that. She was certain there were other things he'd lost, but they simply hadn't discussed them, so she had no idea what those things were.

"Well, get to it." He shook his head. "I'm tired of being wet."

"Listen, Mr. Fussypants, you can go back inside if you want to. I'm going to do this until I figure it out."

He groaned. "That nickname is not sticking. I refuse to allow it."

She smiled. "If the shoe fits, wear it."

Melanie spoke the words from the journal. "The water runs, never stopping. Until now. When I say go, the river will flow in the opposite direction." She paused as the journal said to. "Go."

Pain surged through her veins, like a jolt of electricity. Nausea rocked her, and she almost vomited, but the river switched direction.

"Holy shit!" She walked toward the water, glad she'd managed to keep her food in her stomach.

"What happened?"

"The river, it changed direction."

His mouth fell open. "For real?"

"Yes." She bent over to touch the water. "Did you feel the magic? How awful that felt? It wasn't… natural, not like using my own feels. I've even done other people's spells before and had no problem. This was painful, as though my body revolted from doing it."

He shook his head. "I didn't feel a thing. Can we get the fuck inside?"

She sighed. He was getting testier and testier. Edward had even mentioned it to her this morning. Melanie couldn't remember the last time he'd slept. Even sex didn't tire him out. He just stared at the ceiling all night, seeing nothing but the white in front of his eyes. Frankly, she was shocked he stayed as pleasant as he'd managed to do.

"You should go in. I'm going to watch this for a second. I mean, why have this spell?"

He blinked. "Why have this spell? It's financial, obviously."

There was nothing obvious about it to her, and she was plenty smart. "Explain, please."

He sighed. "Sorry. I… I'm an ass."

She waved her hand. "Don't worry. Financial?"

He walked toward the river, stopping before he almost fell in. "Without water this land is useless." He paused. "Maybe not this land. But the land everywhere. It flows the way it flows and eventually empties out into a basin that is used for distribution to the herb companies, the ones the healers use, for example. Other stuff, too. I don't know because I never paid attention to it, but we own it. Well, I do. No more after me because they're all dead." His face fell. "What color was my mother's hair?"

Melanie rose, touching his shoulder. "Brown. So you own that basin and eventually we could drain the basin if I don't put the river back the way it goes."

"Yes, exactly. The water around here determines a lot of business. Fishing. Where the white water comes from there are tourist places, I'm sure you've seen those. It's small here, but it starts to widen before it gets to that basin. And... there are other things. I can't think of them. Fuck, this is happening a lot, isn't it?"

She nudged him. "Doesn't matter. I don't want you to worry about it. The finances of the river." She turned to look at the house. "So conceivably if I didn't put this back, a lot of people would be out of work, that basin might dry up, the whole economy of the area would change."

"Yes, I guess it could." He ran a hand over his face. "Does that matter?"

"It might." She shivered. "This is not magic anyone should be doing. It feels wrong. I don't like it, and I don't like it in conjunction with your house being loaded up with ghosts."

He scrunched up his nose. "What is the correlation between the two? A bad spell you've found somewhere and the ghosts in my house? They may have nothing to do with each other."

Maybe that was true. Maybe it wasn't. He didn't remember the journal. She didn't think it was a happy accident that the box hidden in the attic with the journal that had this spell was important. At the end of the day, this all came down to money.

Sometimes she just knew things. The law. Who should

date who. And why this whole mess had started in the first place.

It just meant she was going to find a ghost no one could ever see and get some answers.

Melanie squeezed Elliot's hand. None of this necessarily had any bearing on the curse. That was the unfortunate part. She might solve a mystery and it would still have no ability to make what she really wanted fixed any better.

"Give me a second. I have to turn the river back around." Her stomach clenched. "This is going to hurt."

* * *

THE MOONLIGHT TRAVELED through the window, bathing the bedroom in an almost surreal comfort considering the night. Elliot was awake, staring at the ceiling but seeing nothing, and Melanie had almost gotten used to his being that way.

She couldn't sleep and so they shared that for the evening. Mel leaned her head on his shoulder. "You have something on your mind. You're not writing." Most of the time when he was up the pencil moved on the paper, nearly silently, a noise she'd gotten so used to it was almost like white noise at this point.

He sighed. "I think you should go."

Dread filled her. Yes, she'd annoyed him outside by the river by keeping him out in the rain, but the rest of the afternoon had gone pretty well. He'd laughed a little bit, written, and they'd had a nice dinner. "I'm sorry if I've done something but..."

He put his hand on her arm. "No, it's not you. Trust me on that. I'm not even a little bit wanting you to go. I... I want to keep you with me every day that I'm breathing. No, it's that I can see the handwriting on the wall. See what I did there? See?" He gave her his sardonic grin that she loved so much that she had to reach out to touch his lips just to feel it.

He brought her hand to his mouth and kissed it. "Let me finish, Mel. I need you to go before you're in danger here. I know I'm forgetting things. You're being kind about it, and I can hear you doing it. What concerns me is that I will lose the magic and not know it. You'll be exposed; the security spell will be gone. I can't promise that I'll be able to remember to tell you I'm losing it. I think it makes the most sense for you to go while I still can have this much sense inside of me."

She hated that he was right but she wasn't ready. "We have a little time before that happens. I know we do. I promise to leave before we get there, okay?"

He winced. "Honey, I'm not sure you will know. The way it's working with me is so different than my father. How do I know I won't get up tomorrow from this bed and have no idea who you are?"

Her chest ached at that thought. "I need... I need a few more days. I'm not ready. I haven't done what I said I would do, and I'm not ready to say goodbye to you." She wiped away the tears that flooded her eyes. "Because it will be the last time I see you. I know you. Even if you retain your memory, you won't let me back, won't let me see the decline. Please. Not yet. I'm being selfish."

He held her close, drawing her against his chest. "Why did it have to be now? Why couldn't we have found each other five years ago?"

"How could it have been any other time?" She lay across his chest, listening to his heartbeat. "You said it yourself. You never let anyone in."

He ran his fingers through her hair. "I'd have let you in, Mel. I wouldn't have been able to stop it."

No, she couldn't spend another night crying. There was just so much pain in the world that she could tolerate.

He looked over at her. "Where are you going?"

"I'm not going. I'm just summoning a pen and paper. I'm going to write a spell."

"Mel." He shook his head. "We can't both be exhausted. You have to sleep sometime. It's been a long day. You temporarily altered the natural flow of a river."

"What if I didn't? What if someone else altered the natural flow of a river, and I temporarily put it back the way it was supposed to be?" She'd been quietly dwelling on this for hours. "At this point there isn't any changing it. Too many people depend on it to go the way it's going, but what if that was the point of the spell to begin with? I've found"—how to do this without mentioning the journal?—"other spells around the house that seem to all be about altering things, including the creation of magic itself. I'm not even sure what to make of that because how does one create magic? But I digress. What if the river is already running incorrectly?"

"I don't know that rivers run incorrectly in magical places. There are rules in nature for these kinds of things by the humans but there are no rules of nature around us. You know that. But I take your point. We moved in and presumably someone—my family?—altered the river to suit their needs with that unhealthy spell?"

She thought for a second. Was that what she was saying? "Yes, that's it."

"I don't know that there's anything to do about it now. And we'll never really know."

That wasn't true. "We might know." She pointed at the ceiling before she remembered he couldn't see it. Sometimes she just forgot. "The guy in the attic is your ancestor. I just have to stop being unable to see him. So I'm... going to work on it."

He shook his head. "If anyone can figure it out it's you, that's for sure. If you're going to do that, then I'm going to write, too."

She shoved his shoulder. "You were going to do that anyway."

"True."

Melanie stared at him for a second. Dark circles under his eyes marred his face. She hated seeing them because of what they meant. "Do you want to try to sleep?"

"I can't." He shook his head. "Hard to explain except I finally understand what my father meant about the low buzzing he was always hearing. There really is a constant buzz in the air. I can't... between the white light and the buzz, my head won't shut off. It should kill me. People can't go forever without sleep, but it's the curse. It'll keep me alive a long while like this. Just not capable of rational thought. So... there it is."

He didn't tell her anything she didn't know, yet it burned to hear it all the same. Still, this was his pain, and she wouldn't make it harder on him by making this all about her feelings. They'd be right there for her to deal with another time.

In any case, she summoned the notebook she wanted to work in and started writing. Why didn't anyone make up spells outside of school? It was like the entire witching community had gotten lazy. Witches used to invent new spells all the time. Now, it was just a matter of convenience and making things easier on themselves using spells that had been around forever.

In fact, she didn't even recall making up spells in the upper school. It had been all about mastering old ones, committing them to memory, becoming stronger in her own gifts to be better at the predesigned spells. She couldn't remember the last time she'd written one.

Unlike the odd journal she'd examined, she didn't need to write out spells like she was instructing a child how to do them. Impressions would work just fine, assuming her magic didn't have something wrong with it.

House. In her mind, she pictured the house they stayed in. Boothe Estate with its long hallways, huge rooms, and mysteries that only she seemed concerned with uncovering.

That had to be a good place to start.

She chewed on her lip. What was next? She needed to be able to see what she hadn't been able to. Lightning lit up the room a second before thunder struck. She shivered and Elliot reached out to rub her arms.

"You can't see, but you are more attuned to things than anyone I know."

He kissed her neck. "You make me feel like I'm still alive. I wonder if I am, or if I'm just a ghost in this house."

"Oh, my darling." Mel kissed his cheek. "You are very much alive."

Elliot lifted his eyebrows. "That is debatable, although I love the darling. Keep using that."

Leave it to Elliot to defuse a tense moment. "Sure, darling. I'll just shove it on everything, darling. Okay, darling?"

He snorted. "How did I ever get through a night without you, Mel?"

She wasn't sure how she was going to get through future nights. Mel forced herself back to the trial at hand. She needed to write a spell.

She worked at it for what felt like hours but might have been twenty minutes. It was the sound of Elliot snoring that caught her attention and pulled it away. He was asleep. She could have shouted for joy over it, only that would have defeated the purpose and woken him up.

Of course, it might not have. He was out cold. Mel waved

her hand to bring the blanket up around him, and he didn't stir.

She stared down at what she'd written. It really might work. Melanie was just going to have to harness some of her own magic to see if she could make this happen tonight. She got out of the bed as carefully as she could and snuck out of the room, floating.

Melanie used to sneak around the estate doing magic only teenagers experimented with. It was odd little things but forbidden nonetheless. Outside on these grounds she'd once completely altered the length of her hair until it touched the dirt. A bunch of bugs had crawled up in it and that hadn't been fun.

She'd never done that again.

Steeling her shoulders she had to remind herself that she was an adult and as long as her magic hurt no one, there was nothing forbidden to her. Still, she worried her lower lip and didn't rush out to get moving with this spell.

Instead, she waved her hand and sent Ava a message.

Hey, I might be getting ready to do something really dumb. By the time you see this in the morning, after it's gone through the safety channels, my potential dumbness will have already happened. I guess we'll know just how stupid I am.

She sent it off and walked into the center hall. With one last look at the spell she'd created—House, Veil, Eyes, Unseen —she opened herself up to her own magic. It had been a long time since she'd done this. Unlike the river spell, doing so didn't hurt. Some witches did this every day to stay sharp. Her own career hadn't needed her to be physically strong for the sake of magic, and she'd only dabbled with this on occasion. Mostly, right before court.

Her fingers buzzed. This time however, she was going to shut it down and angle the excess energy toward winning an argument, toward being intuitive, anticipating responses, and keeping her mind sharp. No, she focused it right down to the words on the page.

The notebook flipped fast. Well, that had been unexpected. She hadn't wanted that to happen. What was going on?

The room flashed a bright light before it seemed to go black and white and then righted itself again. She sucked in a breath. Anxiety rushed through her, but she pushed it away. What had happened? She wanted to see a ghost not...

Melanie stopped her internal rant and looked around. Everything in this place looked... different. It was hard to put her finger on exactly what was wrong until she noticed the chandelier above her head. When she'd done the spell, the chandelier had been intact. Now, it looked like one of the pieces hung down, swinging. She blinked. That wasn't entirely true. It was like she could see two versions of the chandelier at the same time. One where it was beautiful, dusted, and in one piece. And this version. They both existed together.

She put her hands on her hips. This was so weird. Surely she could come up with a better word than that. Surreal, maybe.

Melanie walked forward. The whole room was doubled. One version was clean, pristine, well looked after, but it was almost like it was a glamour. Like the time she'd grown her hair too long. That hadn't been real. Witches weren't supposed to alter reality for extended periods of time. Things could get fuzzy.

Like this house.

Melanie rushed up the stairs. She had to get to the attic while this still lasted. But before that she wanted to check on Elliot.

What did the doubling do to him?

Melanie rushed into the bedroom and came up short. He

slept as she'd left him, but all around him, sucking the life right out of his body, were ghosts. They had their hands all over him.

She gasped, not even trying to be quiet. "Get away from him."

This time every ghost in the room—and there were dozens—turned to stare at her. Dread filled her soul.

CHAPTER 12

"Get away from him," she shouted again, rushing toward the ghosts. They didn't move. She got even closer, not sure what she was going to do. If she could see them, maybe she could touch them?

That didn't happen. As though there was no one there, her hand went right through the first ghost she tried to grab like they were nothing more than air. Melanie fought back her fear. This was too much. What was happening here? It was like they were feeding off Elliot. Was that part of his curse or the curse itself?

She couldn't make sense of it.

"Melanie," Hannah spoke to her with a soft voice. "Don't forget what you set out to do. I'm counting on you."

The little ghost was counting on her? To do what? Still, it was a reminder. Much as she'd like to stay here and see what she could do for Elliot, she was clueless as to how. There might be answers upstairs in the attic about what she could do down here to protect him.

She touched his forehead. He was warm but not too hot. For now, he'd hang on. She'd be right back. To do what, she wasn't exactly sure, but she'd do something. Fixing problems was what she did.

Melanie floated up fast. She'd always been an adequate flyer but not necessarily going to win any award for doing it. Still, she went as fast as she possibly could and managed to get into the attic. Like everything else, it seemed doubled. Melanie wasn't certain why she was able to manage this without puking. Usually, she got dizzy pretty easily.

It must have been the spell.

But standing in the middle of the attic was a man she'd never seen before. He was still when she came up before he started pacing, back and forth, back and forth. He had his hands in his hair, and she stared at him.

He was shorter than she was and dressed in old-fashioned clothing, although he was only wearing one boot, which was strange enough to catch her attention. She shook her head. Fashion would have to wait.

"Who are you?" she shouted. It hadn't occurred to her until she uttered the words that he might not be coherent. There was the little girl downstairs who could make some kind of sense and then there was the gardener with nothing to say in the present.

He whirled around. "You can see me."

"I can see you."

He clasped his hands together. "You did a spell. Finally, someone did a spell. When I saw you, I knew you were smart."

She swallowed. So this was the coherent kind. That was good and bad. She wanted this, and yet it made her want to vomit. "Who are you?"

"My name is Max Boothe. I did this. I'm responsible for this. Whoever you are… you have to fix this."

She wasn't even a little bit sure she could. "Keep talking."

"I… I wanted to be rich. We were nothing." He took two

steps toward her and gripped his head. "I'm sorry. It's hard for me to talk like this. Everything is always a blinding light. And I lose consciousness."

That sounded familiar. Very much like what was happening to the man she loved. "Elliot goes through that, or similar things."

"I know." He paced again. "All of my descendants have been given the same thing. It's always because of me. Because of what I did. You have to understand... I wanted to be rich."

Melanie tilted her head. Once again, whatever it was about her intuition had been right on. It came down to the money. "You guys weren't rich and you wanted to be. What did you do? Change the river and it did what? Fucked up something inside of you?"

He winced, and she wondered if it was because of what she'd accused him of or because she'd cursed. Her language was probably different than what he'd been used to hearing. Well, she didn't care. Not even a little bit.

"The river was nothing. It was just a first start. I changed the direction, and we harnessed some of that for companies and our own financial interests. Other small things, the way the wind blew. Small things, but we were able to steadily build revenue."

She used to deal with this kind of thing every day. The financial markets had been her specialty for her clients. A touch here, a dash here, keeping the law on their side. She'd always been great at managing these kinds of things. And like the clients she dealt with back then, she knew exactly where this kind of thing was going to go next.

"It wasn't enough money."

He flared his nostrils. "I can't justify it except that we were terrified to be poor. My wife wanted to keep up with the neighbors, and I wanted to beat them. We built this place

149

up, placed wards on it. I even used my wand like an old fashioned heathen."

"And then something happened." She filled in the blank. "To you. To this house."

He visibly swallowed. "Undo it, please. Generation after generation things go terribly wrong. It has killed all my descendants, and I am stuck up here watching. Undo it. Please."

Whatever she would have said, she never got to say because the spell she'd placed on herself wore off. Like the temporary length of her hair when she'd spelled it to grow, it could only stay that way for so long.

Her vision was fading. She'd never be able to see this without the spell, but she wasn't going to just spell herself again. If she was going to do this, then she was going to have to some help. A simple vision spell she could make up, but undoing a spell that controlled the fate of the Boothe family for generations was beyond her.

She needed help.

Melanie turned and ran down the stairs. She couldn't protect Elliot from this, but she could be proactive and get him some people who could help.

"Lawson," she verbally dictated the note as she ran. "I need all of you, and I need you to get in here without setting off the security. Please. Now. As soon as you get this."

The best thing Elliot could do was sleep. The last thing she needed was to wake him up in the middle of this mess. For all she knew, the ghosts were always on him and only some of them were sometimes visible. Maybe she'd get to ask the man in the attic who'd caused this, maybe she wouldn't. Maybe somehow she'd deal with the fact that every time she'd touched him, been intimate with him, the ghosts were probably there. She shuddered. Yeah... she was putting that right away in the category of "cognitive dissonance is a good thing" box.

By the time she got to the bottom of the stairs, Lawson stood there. That didn't surprise her in the least. He'd figured out how to get through Elliot's security. That was what he did.

"Mel? What the fuck?"

She took a deep breath. "I need you to follow me into a very strange path and not act like I'm nuts."

He tilted his head. "Talk."

* * *

SHE STOOD around the table as Eleanor scribbled notes on the notebook in front of her. She'd taken Melanie's original spell and altered it. Or was trying to. It turned out Eleanor really had a skill for this. Next to her, Mitchell oscillated between pacing and rubbing his wife's back.

Everyone else was silent. She didn't blame them. This was a lot to digest. More than she'd imagined it to be.

A spell to make a family richer had gone askew, and now, generations later, there was nothing but tragedy. The question was how had he done it. And for that, they had to ask him. They had to know the right questions to ask.

Kim finally spoke from where she sat in the corner. She didn't feel well, but she was working it out. Melanie was impressed by how tough the other woman seemed to be despite the nausea. Mel hated puking.

"Here's the thing about this curse." Kim rubbed her face. "It moves all over him, which makes sense if what we are seeing is actually ghosts or something draining his energy like a giant sucking leach. Taking a piece of him at a time, as though they need his energy to keep going. But if he is their food source, so to speak, then by doing this, they're taking away the only thing they can feed on. And then they lose what they need."

Mel shuddered. The very idea, even though she'd seen it, was just awful.

Kim stumbled to her feet, and Stefan steadied her. "Sorry, most women get sick in the morning. I'm middle of the night. So I'm doing the best I can here."

Stefan nudged her. "Want to go home?"

"No. I want to finish my thought." She groaned. "The curse will protect itself. It's like a living creature. Try and kill it, it will fight back."

Melanie grasped what was not being said. "The only thing it can fight back against is Elliot. But why would it want to? I mean… do you kill your only source of food?"

"You do, if you think it's going to go away. You get as much as you can."

Lawson knocked his fingers on the table. "Give me something to destroy, and I'll destroy it."

Eleanor floated up the paper. "Maybe we can all see it this way."

"We need to exorcise the ghosts. Maybe we do it the human way." Stefan met Eleanor's gaze. "What do you think?"

Eleanor shook her head. "It's not what I think. Not really. It's what Elliot thinks, or if he's not capable of making this kind of decision, it's what Mel thinks."

"What I think?" Melanie wasn't certain she had the right to do that. "I'm not his wife. Even if he weren't cursed, I don't think I'd be that. He'd have met someone in all of those years out there and never have met me. We have something but it might just be because of the curse."

Ava wrapped her arms around her. "What difference does that make really? We aren't remaking the past. Even with all the magic in this room, we can't do that. What happened, happened. You love each other. So you can decide if he can't."

As if on cue, Elliot stumbled into the room. He held his head, and with her heart stuttering, Mel ran over to him. "Hey, are you okay?"

He jolted backward. "Who are you? Who's here?"

She swallowed. "It's Melanie. And I've brought Lawson and the others here. We have an idea of how to help."

Elliot paled. "Melanie who? I… I don't know who you are. Any of you. Who are you? Who… who am I? Why can't I see?"

Coldness wafted over her. He'd been fine before he fell asleep, or still relatively coherent. It had taken years for his father to get to this point. How could it have been a matter of hours?

Still, he was terrified and that was the most important thing right now. As long as he was alive and talking they could get this thing off of him and then the healers could do what they did.

"That's okay. Listen, you're not well right now. Be calm. Let's sit down."

He shook his head, backing into the wall behind him. "Something is very wrong."

She whirled around. "Let's do whatever we need to do to make this happen. Exorcism. Whatever. Make the spell happen. There are probably ghosts all over him right now."

Mitchell waved his hand in the air. "Everyone in a circle. No, Ava, Kim, out of here. I don't want these ghosts messing with your pregnancies. This is all new to me, and I'm making it up as I go along."

Kim nodded, grabbing onto Ava's hand and leading her out the door. They were gone just as Elliot doubled over. That couldn't be a good sign. Maybe the ghosts seeing her had caused just what Kim had predicted and they doubled down their attack on him.

She put her hand on his back. What she wanted to do was hold him but he didn't know her, and she wasn't his wife. Consent wasn't necessarily implied when it wasn't given.

"Hold on for me. Okay? Please believe we are here to help you. I promise you that."

Eleanor seemed to be uttering something under her breath. A wave of magic passed through Mel, and the world blurred and then doubled again.

Lawson blinked rapidly. "Fuck me. I wasn't sure I believed this would happen. This is lunacy. Okay. Upstairs we go to talk to that dude."

Elliot called out again. She didn't know if they had time for talking. Melanie grabbed off the table that Mitchell had been looking at. The ghosts had to be gotten rid of and that included the man upstairs. She didn't want to have a whole additional rundown. Lawson could talk to the man. He and Stefan ran upstairs.

She was getting rid of these things.

The book was blurry, but her eyes adjusted. She'd figure out what caused that later when she could actually consider this thing from start to finish.

Humans said words to exorcise demons. They made it seem like it was a religious thing and that was well above her pay grade. Witches were different, but they'd certainly agree that words held power. All of this had started from that.

A man wanted more money, more power, reputation. But boy had it spiraled out of control. Be careful what you wish for—that was something humans said. Witches had their own expression. Be careful what spell you cast.

Well, she'd only started casting again today. Fuck, she'd have to be good enough. She turned to stare at Elliot. He was covered in the ghosts. The poor man. They were going to kill him. But she loved him, and regardless of the circumstances of how they came together, she wasn't yet ready to let him go.

"Elliot, I'm in love with you. You don't remember me because you're sick. That doesn't change anything."

He lifted his head like he wanted to say something before falling to his knees.

No, she wouldn't lose him to this thing. She'd found that fucking journal. Words. That was all that she needed.

She started talking, as fast as she could, anything she could think of that might work. It was the intent behind them that mattered.

This was like a disease, and she would beat it. She just had to remember that the point of magic was your intent.

She awakened her magic. It was hard, much tougher than it should have been, but if she got Elliot through this mess, she was going to see to it that she got back to basics when it came to magic. She was going to remember what it meant to be a witch.

Melanie had to think about the kind of magic that automatically made her own turn on. Solving problems was something that always did that for her. She thought about Evans and the fact that she was still stuck in this house because of him. There had to be a solution to that, something she'd been putting off, because the truth was she'd liked being trapped here with Elliot. She'd liked that she couldn't leave, that she had him to herself. But much as she did, this had to stop.

Her powers turned on, hard. She jolted. Nothing, not even making the vision spell, had been the equivalent of this. Maybe it was adrenaline or perhaps it just came down to the pressing need to get this done.

She cleared her throat. "I want to see what's on you, and I want the ability to touch them to move them, to feel the unfeelable." That was just pathetic, but so help her, it was going to have to do. "Seeing. Touching. Feeling." She loved this man, so she infused the words with that too.

It was possible to make something mean more by simply staring at the person she loved while she uttered those words. In her whole life, Melanie had never known that. This was why people went to jail for illegal magic when they had been law abiding citizens. She'd never understood it, might never again. But for the first time in her life, she could actually comprehend why people committed crimes for those they loved.

In that moment, she'd have broken every magical law imaginable to rid Elliot of this curse.

"Melanie," he spoke through gritted teeth. "I can't keep you safe. You need to go."

How did he know her? It wasn't possible. Once they lost their memories, the Boothes didn't get them back, and yet he hadn't known her and now he did.

"Elliot, I'm not going anywhere. We've figured it out, and we're fixing this."

He shook his head. "I love you. I've held on for you when I should have vanished weeks ago. Please don't stay here too long."

She leaned over and kissed him on his forehead. "I've got this. Please trust me."

"I do." He took her hand. "But I need for you to listen to me for one second before I lose the words to say this again."

She almost begged him to stop, to not say whatever it was he thought he had to, because she knew beyond a shadow of a doubt that it was going to be too close to goodbye. "Go ahead."

"Mel, you are not too much. You always say that, but you're not. You're nowhere near too much of anything."

She didn't know what he was talking about. "What?"

"That thing you say? That you're too much? You're not. There is no part of you that is too much. You are just right. Strong. Brilliant. Capable. Stop thinking you are too much. If he can't love you the right way, he's too little. He's not enough. Not the other way around."

Mel ignored the lump in her throat and kissed him again. "We can talk about this later."

"I don't think we can." He kissed her square on the lips. "I'm going, Mel. And I don't know that I'm ever coming back."

Tears rushed down her cheeks, and she didn't try to hide them. "You're not going anywhere, Elliot Boothe. I forbid it."

He laughed, which was highly inappropriate for the moment, but it was so Elliot that it made her grin. How was he even doing this? "You were gone, you didn't know me."

"It's a void, Mel. I can't explain it. I pushed through it, but I don't think I can again. I'll just be... lost to it. I love you."

There had never been such powerful words. Yes, those were what she needed. She pushed into the spell she'd made in her head. Ghosts. Visible. Touchable. Beatable. All of it made her body buzz like she'd jolted herself with electrical current.

She waved her hand. Damn it, this had to work.

Stefan popped into the room. "I was talking to the one upstairs and... shit, what did you do? I can feel the magic in here. That's strong stuff. Did you do that, Mel?"

She nodded. "I did."

More, she was absolutely certain it worked because she could see the ghosts again. But this time they weren't translucent. She reached out and yanked on the arm of one woman sucking on Elliot's energy and actually managed to dislodge her.

Elliot groaned. "Fuck me. What was that?"

That was right. He still didn't know. "Ghosts. I'm taking ghosts off of you."

He winced. "Why are they on me?"

"That's a very long story. But we are all here trying to fix it."

Elliot grabbed her hand. "Get out of here, Melanie. If there is something happening in this house you need to get away from here."

That was the problem. It wasn't just this house. If that had been the case, she would have taken Elliot and run from here as fast as she could, never looking back. No, this would follow him, and she wasn't going to leave him.

"Tell you what. When this is over we'll both go see a Bomber play. How does that sound?"

He shook his head. "Who?"

Well, that wasn't good. Not at all. "Never mind. I'm not leaving."

Intent, she needed to remember that it all came down to that. In her law life, that had been true. They'd taken it from the humans, or at least that was what the histories said had happened. Did the witch who cursed another witch have murderous intent? Probably not in this case. He'd wanted to be a rich man; he'd never imagined the suffering that his desires would unleash on everyone.

How many people would die in terrible agony, some of them getting stuck here to feed off of his descendants like leeches? She'd let Eleanor explain to her later how that happened.

For now, she had to think.

"Be gone, ghosts." She pointed at them and nothing happened.

Elliot lifted his head to stare at her. "Be gone ghosts?"

Right, that was pretty stupid. She could do better than

that. Stefan ran next to her. "We have to get rid of the curse, of what he did to begin with."

Stefan whirled his hand in the air. "What was changed, undo."

That was a good start. The house groaned and Elliot held onto his head. "What is going on?"

She rushed to the window and stared outside. It was hard to tell, but she would swear the river was rushing the other way. That had to be a good sign. The problem was the ghosts were still here so it was clearly not going to just be that simple. Nausea roiled through her. This was the same feeling as the last time she'd made the water rush the other way. There was just a general feeling of wrongness.

"The forces here don't want to be gotten rid of." She bit down on her lip. "What shouldn't be here," she practically shouted in the direction of the ghosts, her voice raising with every word she spoke, "needs to go. Be gone. You're over."

The house shook, and as she watched, a hole seemed to open in the ceiling. Wind whipped around, and she backed up, instinct making her move before she forced herself to do the opposite. Fear wasn't going to dictate her life anymore. She rushed forward, wrapping her arms around Elliot, which was harder than it should have been because she could actually see the ghosts.

Next to her the female ghost's eyes widened. She looked at Melanie. "Thank you."

Thank you? Melanie wasn't even sure what to say about that. Elliot shook as each ghost floated away, into that hole, leaving the house. Lawson popped into the room. "What did you do, Stefan? It's working."

"Not me. She did this."

She held on tighter. "It's almost over." She didn't actually know this, but she was going to say it and hope that her luck stayed on point the way it had. Intention. She had it in abundance.

And just like that, it was over. The ghosts were gone. The house was quiet, and Elliot was still in her arms. She kissed his cheek, once then twice. "Baby, it's done."

He didn't answer, so she pulled back to stare at him. "Elliot?"

Even as she spoke, she could see the truth. He stared at her, breathing, his heart beating, but his eyes saw nothing and his mind... was gone.

She'd broken the curse, sent the ghosts away, and all of it had been too long for Elliot... he'd held on, pushed back from the void, but he was gone now.

Melanie sobbed, dropping his arm to cover her mouth. Lawson knelt down next to her. "Mel?"

"He's gone."

"We have to get out of here, you're exposed."

She shook her head, fast. "I don't care."

Right then, the entirety of Evans' empire could come and find her. She didn't give a shit.

CHAPTER 13

So many things happened in utter silence that Mel could hardly believe they were happening at all. She sat on the floor next to Elliot. He stared straight ahead. Nothing had changed nor would it. She rubbed his hand in her own.

The place swarmed with Enforcers. That was Lawson's doing. She was exposed. The location spell that Evans had on her would be visible now. She put her head on her knees. Elliot was here, but he was gone.

He'd pushed through the void for her once but this was different. She could feel it. He wasn't here.

Ava knelt down in front of her. "How are you doing?"

"You should go home. You've been up all night."

Ava tilted her head to the side. "You're coming with us. You'll stay with us until this is over."

She'd been so fearful when this whole thing began. Attacked by an assassin, she'd hardly known what was up or what was down. Oh, who was she kidding? She'd been fearful before that. From the day she'd stepped foot in school and found out there were people for whom she would never be good enough simply because of some status hierarchy, Melanie had lived her whole life afraid.

Elliot would have probably called that a tragedy. Or he'd have put the storyline in a play that he might never get credited for having written.

No, she wasn't doing this anymore.

"What will Lawson do with Elliot? Someone should call Edward. We've skipped over the raving madness and gone straight to brain death. Edward must know what Elliot wanted in this situation."

Ava sighed. "You're always working out the logistics of things. Even when we're trying to do them for you."

"Ava..."

"No, don't answer me. You asked me a question. I'm frustrated because my heart is breaking for you as I watch yours break, and I can't fix this. But this isn't about me. It's about you, and I'd want to know, too. Lawson spoke to Edward. Elliot wanted to be sure he was kept comfortable without physical pain while he waited for this to be over. Not that he could necessarily feel anything. But Lawson has a good relationship with a healer. She's going to take him on in her private clinic. And it will likely not be long."

Mel got to her feet. "Thank you for that. And... thank you for the offer to stay. I'm afraid I'm going to have to decline."

"Declining isn't really an option," Lawson said from across the room. "You're coming home with us."

No, she wasn't. Melanie bent over and kissed Elliot lightly on the mouth. "I love you, and I will always miss you. We made the curse go away. I'm sorry it was too late. But no one else will ever suffer."

She stepped forward. "I'm sorry, Lawson. I'm not going with you. I have something to do. I'm under arrest for nothing. I know that you have worked tirelessly on my behalf.

You guys have all protected me, endlessly. I am grateful beyond my capacity for words…"

"Mel," Ava tried to interrupt her, but she kept going.

"I have something to do. And I'm not going to hide from it anymore."

She couldn't pop in and out but maybe it was something on her face, maybe it was the way she looked at him, but not one Enforcer chased her from the room when she left. Grief rolled her hard. She could hardly believe that she had the capacity to keep her head up. Still, she wouldn't fall apart, not until after she had put Peter Evans to bed.

* * *

SHE STORMED to Peter Evans home and knocked on the door. It took him a minute to answer, which didn't surprise her. If he had banged on her door, she'd have taken a minute to figure out what the fuck to do, too.

This man had sent an assassin after her. She was fully aware that she took her own life in her hands doing this and it was likely a stupid move, maybe even one that would get her killed. Still, there were things to be said and she was tired of hiding.

"Ms. Syed." He was taller than she was, and as he opened the door, speaking her name, she had to stretch her neck back to look at him.

"Mr. Evans," she answered him. "I'm not going to hide anymore, and you aren't going to try to kill me."

He didn't answer right away. "I never tried to have you killed."

That was good. This would have been too easy if he'd confessed. Boom. Confession. The whole thing over. When did anything really work out like that?

"Okay. Fine. We'll say a person who might want to kill me is going to stop right now."

He took a long pause before he spoke. "Why would a person do that?"

"Well, I'd assume that if a person wasn't a total jackass they'd have by now moved their money from where I found it in the first place. Since I am turning over a new leaf and completely disinterested in continuing as I had, I can assure that person that I won't be going looking for any more money that may or may not belong to the person who wanted to kill me. I was only doing that to help your former wife to begin with."

He opened and closed his mouth, so she kept speaking. "I spent a lot of time trying to figure out why you did the things that you did. Why did you marry so many women and divorce them? That isn't what we do as witches. We share souls. We marry once, and it's for life. It's such a strange occurrence for a witch to even cheat. And yet you marry and divorce. Marry and divorce."

She stepped to the side to get a look inside of his house. It was dark, but she could see all the way to the living room, which was barrenly decorated. One couch, nothing else catching her eye.

"No one else ever gave you a problem. I get that. She went to me, she broke the rules, didn't use your appointed lawyer to handle the divorce. I know the firm you use. They're as crooked as they come."

He flared his nostrils. "You're skating on thin ice, Ms. Syed."

"We don't really skate as witches, much, do we? I mean... I guess we just kind of fly over it. Never mind. That is neither here nor there. She came to me, and I was actually giving her legitimate counsel. We were going to get the compulsion spell that kept her from talking off of her. The secrets were going to spill right out. You couldn't have that."

Adrenaline raced through her veins, making her feel elated. If she lived through this, she was going to crash. Hard. Between this and the grief, she might not get up for a week. But she did this for Elliot as much as anything else. He had never gotten to live his life; he'd had a burden not of his own making riding him the whole time. If he'd taught her anything, it was that she wasn't going to live hers looking over her shoulder because some madman had it out for her. After today, she'd always see him just as he truly was: a whole bunch of nothing special.

"I asked myself over and over... was it about the money? She hadn't been married to you very long. She wasn't going to be entitled to half of your estate, and the minimum amount of money you'd have owed her, you'd have made up in no time. It couldn't be the money, and I don't believe a person as successful as you in business would have made the mistake of sharing secrets with a person you knew you'd be willing to discard. So what was it?"

He was red in the face now. "And you think you know, do you?"

"Yes I do." She really did. Clarity had hit her as she'd sat on the floor with Elliot, his eyes forever unseeing. "It's hard to be a witch. I know that is a ridiculous thing to say, but it really is. Almost since birth, we're all preoccupied with finding our soul mates. It seems very important to us. We need someone to share our souls with. We're made to have it. And then if it doesn't come, it can come to feel a little bit like... desperation."

He shook his head. "I have never been desperate for anything in my entire life."

"You lied when you said you didn't order me killed, and now you've lied again. That's two lies. That's fine. I didn't expect you to admit to it. But the years as they passed and she—whoever that she is that you're supposed to have—didn't present herself, that must have made you feel nuts. You're a rich, good looking, powerful, successful man who has everything. Except your soul mate. You must have thought you could force it. That somewhere along the line you'd meet someone who would at least do. Someone you could force to fit in the box."

She stepped toward him. Her powers rode her. This was what it felt like in court when she was winning. Melanie had him. She knew she did.

"So you get these women who need money and power, or maybe they just have daddy issues, to agree to take that spell with you, to bind their souls. Only it doesn't work, does it? Something feels awful inside. You aren't meant to be together. You're not right. And it must just feel sickening. Like… a person changing the direction of a river, it's unnatural magic."

He made a face, and she wasn't surprised. He wouldn't have the slightest idea what she meant and that was fine. It had all become clear to her, like clouds moving away from her vision to let in the light of day.

"You have to undo it. You divorce. But you can't have them talking because no one can know just how desperate and sad and… lonely you are. That would ruin everything. No one can ever know. But I do. That's why you want to kill me, right? Because, I see you just as you are. Just the way that Elaine, your poor dead wife, did. Sad. Lonely. Not worthy of a soul mate."

He pointed his finger at her. "You're dead. I called the assassins before I answered the door. You're dead. You'll never make it out of here alive."

She tilted her head. "Get that Lawson?"

The Enforcer popped next to Evans, Stefan on the other

166

side. The former nodded. "Sure did. You're coming with me, Mr. Evans. Threats against a member of the court are punishable by vanishing from existence. My colleague is going to show you your new home."

Melanie had the pleasure of watching the man pale before Stefan took him away.

Lawson stared at her. "That was quite a risk you just took."

"I knew you would follow." And right now she didn't care about taking risks, about whether or not she made it out of anything. She'd like to think that there would be a time when maybe she would feel differently again but that wasn't going to be anytime soon.

Now there was just the absence of Elliot.

Lawson sighed. "You know you're our family. You're not alone."

"I appreciate that." She sighed. "But right now there is only pain. We both know that if you guys didn't care about me, you would have used me as bait a long time ago. I should have drawn him out days ago. Now, it's done. And I guess I'm a hypocrite, because I don't care even a little bit that neither he nor the assassin who is coming up behind me any second won't get a trial."

Lawson waved his hand and the assassin floated into the air. "You felt him?"

"I did. Whatever we did in that house with the ghosts? I feel like it woke up my powers."

"They're buzzing pretty strongly. You know that means you're going to crash."

She stepped back. "I loved him, Lawson. It was only days and maybe it never would have happened if he'd had a normal life, but I loved him nonetheless."

"I know you did. I could feel it. Like I feel it with Eleanor and Mitchell, like I feel it with Kim and Stefan. Like

I know Ava loves me. It's part of what I do. He loved you, too."

"I've got to figure out what to do next."

He nodded. "We're here for you."

She was lucky in her friends, in her family, but that didn't make her any less alone or the lack of Elliot—the sheer absence of his light in her life—any less difficult to deal with. Without Elliot Boothe there was a big gaping hole in the universe.

* * *

ELEANOR LAY on the grass with Melanie, staring up at the afternoon sky. Mel had hardly been alone since everything went wrong. Someone was always with her and that spoke volumes about just how worried about her they all were.

"It was a spell gone terribly wrong. Max, Elliot's ancestor, wanted to be rich. He called a spell of good fortune on the family. But everything has a price. Magic is balance. They had their good fortune, but they also had to live with dying like that."

She jolted at the word. Dead. "And the ghosts? Were they just there or did they come with the spell?"

"When he screwed with the natural forces over there, he made everything a mess. Ghosts. It's just… mind blowing. They are opening a department at Mitchell's university to study ghosts now. Everything about what we thought we knew has changed. Max must have tried to undo things, over and over, while he was still alive. And he just screwed with the natural forces of that entire area. The house, the grounds, it was a plethora of psychic activity. Everything was stuck, like the owner himself."

She supposed that made as much sense as anything in their

lives did. All she had known was that it was a place where she'd fallen in love and lost everything. "Is he gone? Did Lawson tell you guys anything? I'm… I'm not allowed to see him. Edward says Elliot was very specific, no visitors at this stage."

Eleanor shook her head. "I haven't heard anything. I think when Lawson does, you'll be the first to know. I can't imagine him telling anyone else first. Or keeping it from you."

"I'm going back to the house. I promised him I'd get it in order, and I didn't yet. I have to at least do that much for him."

Her friend turned her head. "Do you want help?"

"No. This is something I have to do alone."

* * *

BOOTHE ESTATE FELT EMPTY, and not just because no one was home. It was empty of the life that had made it feel loved. Even when it had been haunted and sucking the life out of Elliot, this place had felt alive. Now, it was cold and empty. Like Melanie on the inside.

She couldn't feel anything.

But that worked fine for what she had to do. With nothing to bother her and her mind on autopilot, she went and ahead and finished cataloging the house. Piece-by-piece, paper-by-paper, things were saved or discarded. The house itself was in perfect shape to be donated to the historical society Elliot had wanted.

The only thing that had to happen was that Elliot had to die. Nothing could happen until then.

"Don't zap me." Edward caught her attention from behind. "I heard you had been here for days. I thought I might be able to help."

She shook her head, turning to regard him. "Zapping is not one of my powers."

"Well, who knows with you? You did all kinds of things from what I heard."

With one last look around, she walked toward Edward. "I still haven't crashed from it. It's like I can feel it coming but then it doesn't."

"You're very strong, Melanie, and you loved him. Grief can and will do strange things to us. Like when I lost my parents. I was… despondent. Elliot picked me up from that mess. Gave me a job and a purpose. And then you found love for me. What makes it great is I think, even though I tried to mind my own business, you found love together. I can't tell you how happy it makes me, the kind of joy it brings to me, to think that he had that before he died. He never thought he should, that he deserved it."

She had to look away from him. "Edward…"

"I know it has left you with a ton of pain. But you made his life full in his last days. That is something to hold onto."

She nodded at him, tears clogging her throat. Melanie really hoped he understood why she couldn't talk anymore.

* * *

ELLIOT

His head hurt, and it seemed like every minute it got worse and worse. He had to do something about it, which meant he had to push through the nothingness that was forever trying to engulf him.

But he wouldn't let it. Melanie had forbidden him from getting lost in the void. He'd held onto that. It was such a strange thing, but it was like he always wanted to do what she said, he always wanted to make her happy.

He pushed and pushed. Sounds came blasting toward his ears. He didn't know if people were shouting, but it certainly sounded like they did.

"I'm telling you, Lawson, there is activity happening in his soul. I can feel it."

Silence followed that statement. Elliot didn't know that voice. It was female but unknown to him. Unless he'd forgotten her. But he didn't think so. Trapped where he was, all the things he had lost were back. He could remember his life.

Finally, Lawson—who he did know although he'd never seen with his eyes—answered. "After a year? Michaella, is that likely? I mean, we knew this could take some time. It took his father years to die; he lingered in incoherence, and Elliot skipped that part, but is that possible?"

She stepped toward. "His body is healthy. I've kept him fed magically. His muscles remain strong. All magic. He could come back and be fine."

A year? Panic filled him, and he drove his consciousness forward. It wasn't something he'd been able to do before now. But desperation made men perform greater feats than this. He surged forward, finally opening his eyes and sitting up. Light blared in on him. Fuck. He could see. Sort of. It wasn't the blinding nothingness of the bright light that had taunted him for years. No, his eyes worked.

A woman he didn't know stared down at him, her mouth gaping open, while a dark haired man—Lawson? —stared at him from the other side.

"Hi." He looked between them. "Sorry, I'm... Elliot, and I think..."

"You've been sick." The woman placed a gentle hand on his arm. "I've been taking care of you. Well, me and a staff of people I employ. My name is Michaella Addington. You've been here and we've been taking care of you."

He nodded. That much he'd gleamed. He knew that name. Addington. They'd run in the same society, well their parents had. He shook his head. That didn't matter right now. Okay. This Michaella person was a healer. That was good. He turned to Lawson who nodded to him.

"Welcome back. This is unexpected. Can you see me?"

He nodded. "I can. You're Lawson. We've had dinner. Spent time together. Did you guys get the curse off of me?"

"Not me. Not Michaella, she took care of you. She's the best, but we thought we were just doing end of life care. No one thought there was a possibility that you could make it. Melanie saved you. She got rid of the curse, cleared the house. It was all her."

My heart rate sped up. My Melanie was amazing. "How did she do that?"

"Force of will. The woman is smart. I always knew that. We used to compete in school, but I think even I underestimated just how smart the woman is."

He swallowed. "Is she okay?"

Elliot wanted to see her more than anything in the universe.

"She's..." Lawson ran a hand through his hair. "Changed. Losing you was a blow I'm not sure she's entirely going to come back from."

No, that wasn't true. She hadn't lost him. He was still here, and he'd spend the rest of his life showing her that he was always going to be around. Elliot jumped out of the bed.

"Whoa," Michaella said, grabbing his arm. "Take it easy. You're very strong, even for being magically helped. But I don't want you to overdo it."

He owed this woman a huge debt. "I see you wear a wedding ring." Three of them around her neck and one on her finger. He didn't know what that was about, and he wasn't going to comment in any case. "What wouldn't you do for the man you're married to?"

Her smile was fast. "Now that is a can of worms you don't want to open. But yes, your point is taken. Come on. Let's get you ready to go get your girl."

Lawson cleared his throat. "That isn't going to be so easy."

Dread filled Elliot's stomach. He'd been gone for a year. Lawson said she was changed. What did that mean? She was so beautiful that men seemed to be unable to stay away from her. Had she married someone else? Was that it? Was she gone from him forever?

"What happened?" He found his voice and forced himself to use it.

Sighing, Lawson answered." There is this whole new field of study in ghosts, because of what happened with you. Melanie has gone back to school, and she's getting her degree in historical witching society with a focus in ghosts. In the meantime, she's left for the summer with several of her professors. She's somewhere… I'm not sure where. I should know. But we have a new baby, and Mitchell and Eleanor went with her. Mitchell is heading up the team. So I know they were in Egypt, but I think they might now be somewhere in China."

China. Okay. Well, that wasn't Mars. He could get to China. "How can we find out exactly where she is? Who would know? Your wife… No, you guys just had that baby. Her mother. I guarantee that Mel's mother knows exactly where she is. Can you find out? Don't tell her about me. I want to speak to Mel before anyone else does. Okay? I don't want her hearing I'm awake from someone else."

Lawson nodded. "In person is always best when you're going to lay your heart on the line." The other man lifted his brows. "Not to state the obvious here, but you've never technically seen Melanie with your eyes. Not as an adult. Is this

173

secrecy because you want a chance to see if you like what she looks like first?"

He walked over to Lawson, somehow managing to keep his back straight and his muscles firm. "What she looks like doesn't matter to me. Not even a little bit. I love her soul. She's beautiful, whatever is there on the outside."

Lawson patted him on the back. "This works out and you're going to be eating at my house every week, Bomber."

"I knew you'd figured it out." There had just been something at the table that night at dinner that tipped Elliot off.

Michaella looked between them. "Am I missing something?"

Lawson shook his head. "Just an old nickname."

So he wasn't going to out him? Maybe Lawson was a man who understood secrets.

CHAPTER 14

ELLIOT

*I*t had taken a week to find her and that was with the help of the Enforcers. Elliot had been right that Mel's mother knew where she was supposed to be. Only she hadn't been there. Apparently, academics did what they did with little regard for men who were supposed to be dead chasing down graduate assistants to confess their love. They chased the history. In this case, that was ghost hunting. Or so he had heard. He hadn't actually seen anyone to discuss it yet.

But she was supposed to be around the corner. Elliot strode through a cave, ducking to watch his head when it got low and getting stares from undergraduates who probably wondered who the dude in the inappropriate clothes was. The rest of them seemed to be in a uniform of some kind of coveralls and smocks that kept them from really brushing up against anything in their clothes.

These caves were old and not viewable to humans. You had to have magic to get inside. That was what Mitchell had told him when he'd met him by the entrance. He'd recognized Mitchell from all of the news footage from when he'd left Ava, Lawson's wife, at the altar years earlier. He hadn't remembered when he'd been blind, hadn't been able to picture him, but it had come back. The poor guy—he was so glad they'd gotten that hex of off him and that they were all happy now and with the right people.

Elliot stopped by the entrance to the small cavern where Mitchell had said Melanie would be. He stood and really looked at her for the very first time. It didn't feel like the first time he'd seen her, even though it was. It would have been hard to explain it to anyone who asked, but it felt like he'd seen her with his heart forever now. Maybe it was because he'd seen her when she was little, but he preferred to think of it as her being such a part of him that he'd already known what she looked like.

And yet... she was so beautiful that she took his fucking breath away, and it was like his eyes got to appreciate her for the first time.

She was turned away from him slightly, looking to her left. Her hair fell slightly out of a messy bun she had at the top of her head. It was more auburn than he would have pictured it, but then he tilted her head and it seemed almost chestnut with gold. He leaned his head against the side of the wall and watched her. He'd known how soft her locks were. His hands tingled for wanting to touch her.

Elliot knew her curves well, the long slope of her neck, the way that her hips felt pressed against his. Her face was beautiful, almost ethereal, like she was from another world. Melanie seemed to glow, and it wasn't about her magic.

It had been a year, and she'd been on her own. Would she even want him back? This was the aching, nagging fear that rode him this week. What if she said no? What if it had all been too much and she didn't want another moment of it?

He stepped toward her, slowly but not silently. She ran a hand through her hair but didn't look up from where she studied the wall paintings. "Did you get the rub? We need to make a sketch of it."

She was obviously not speaking to him. He cleared his throat, suddenly finding it dry. "No, I'm afraid I didn't know you needed any."

Melanie visibly swallowed but didn't turn. Her hand went out to touch the wall as though she needed to steady herself. "I... I wondered if I would see you. All this searching for ghosts. I wondered if after you died if you'd show up. Elliot, I..."

He moved faster than he'd planned, tugging her against him. "I'm not dead. I know it's highly unlikely this would happen. But Mel, I'm here. I woke up."

She shuddered, and when she lifted her head to stare at him, they were with the most wounded brown eyes he'd ever seen. His heart stuttered. Never again. She wouldn't look like this ever again, not in this kind of pain, not if he had anything to say about it.

With a shaking hand, she touched the side of his face. "How? They told me no. They told me... it was going to be over."

"I know they did." He tugged her closer. "It should have been. But you told me I wasn't allowed to leave, and I hung onto that. In the void. I just kept trying and then eventually it worked. I came back."

She cried out, the smallest sound. "Why—Why didn't anyone tell me?"

"I had to come find you myself. I had to tell you." He pulled back just to brush her hair off her forehead. "I had to. Mel, I... I missed you."

Tears leaked from her eyes. "Oh, Elliot. I'm sorry. I'm so sorry I failed you." What was she talking about? He would have asked her if she hadn't rapidly fired the next statement. "I tried so hard and then you were dead... or not dead. Trapped there. And I didn't know. And that is awful. Horrendous. Oh, I..."

He kissed her square on the lips. She closed her eyes a second before he did. For just a moment, they stayed like that. She tasted just the way he remembered, like cherries. Elliot didn't press his kiss harder, this was just a taste, just a new beginning, if she said yes. He wasn't going to ruin it by going too fast. She was wounded, so much more so than he could have imagined, which he couldn't because the equivalent would have been to lose her, and he was unable to fathom such pain.

"Melanie Syed," he whispered in her ear. "I love you so much. And you failed at nothing. I'm only here because you saved me. You did that. And look, I got to come and be all gallant and find you, so thanks for setting me up to look so good."

She laughed. He loved that sound. It moved right through him. He wasn't inherently funny, and yet she did seem to find his weird sense of humor amusing. That was just one of the millions of things he loved about her.

"I love you, Mel. I love you completely."

Her eyes widened. "Oh, Elliot." She tugged a hand free and touched her nose, then her hair. "I look... you've never seen me before and I look... I look like this."

He blinked. "Like what?"

"I'm wearing an apron and my hair is covered in dust. My face is covered in soot." He didn't see any soot. "Elliot, this is the first time you're seeing me and I—"

"Am the most beautiful person I've ever seen. I mean it. I want to look at you every second of every day. I loved you before I could see you. I love you now. I love you. I know it's been a year and things have changed." He motioned toward the cave paintings. "I need to hear about all of them. Do you still... do you still want me after everything that happened? Or was it too much?"

She wrapped her arms around his neck. "I love every bit of your living, breathing self. I... This year has been hell. I tried to change, to make a better show at this crazy life. To not be a constant walking tragedy of pathetic. But I was just pretending. I went from too much to not enough, and I don't know if I can get it all back right away."

He kissed the edge of her nose. "I've got to find my feet, too. How about we do that together?"

She wiped her eyes. "I love you. Love you and you're here." She kissed him, and suddenly, he could have done anything in the universe because she did. "Yes, let's find it together. Please. Oh but I have to stay here. I have to stay on this trek for another few months."

That was fine. "Do you think that Mitchell would mind if I tagged along. I could write. Feed you. Not get in the way but be there and..."

She kissed his chin. "You'd never be in the way. Lots of the graduate students have families with them. Yes, stay with me. And..."

He lifted his eyebrows. "And what? Anything. Name it. There is literally nothing you can't have."

She wrapped his arms around his neck. "You have ten dates to ask me to marry you. Ten." She held up that many fingers. "I know this is very presumptuous of me to say. You're not into marriage. I know this. So you have ten dates for you to decide you want that and ask me. Ten. I've lived a year without you. I want to bond souls. I want... I think you could want it, too."

"Of course, I want it. Do you want me to ask you right now?" How could she think otherwise? "I didn't want it before because of things, but I have to tell you, if I'd met you before the curse took me, I'd have wanted it then, too."

Melanie closed her eyes, sagging a little bit against him, her forehead on his shoulder. "Mel?"

"Sorry, I feel like I can't stay upright. Ten dates. Ten times to take me out."

Ten. He held her close. "Got it, and I've got you. I promise. Forever."

* * *

MELANIE

She loved to watch him sleep in the morning. It was a strange thing, but the moments before he opened his eyes and looked at her were the best in the world because the anticipation was so sweet. His eyes were going to be clear when he opened them, blue with specks of green. He'd smile at her, and he'd be there.

These days, Elliot slept soundly, peacefully, except for the nights when he wrote in his sleep. That hadn't been a cursed thing. That was an Elliot thing.

As if thinking it created the activity, a piece of paper floated into the air next to her. A pencil appeared, and she smiled. Bomber was back to making masterpieces, even in his sleep. She leaned on the pillow, watching his peaceful face. Sometimes he had nightmares. Sometimes she did. And sometimes they both did.

But last night had been peaceful.

The paper floated down in front of her. That was weird. It usually just landed on his desk. She took it, staring at the words in the early morning light. What had he been working on just now?

Hey, baby. I know last night was just date 8 and you told

me 10 dates, but I've never been very good at waiting. Will you marry me?

She gasped, and he laughed, rolling her over until he was on top of her, both of them nearly falling off the bed. "So will you? Marry me? Soon?"

Mel nodded, joy warring with her constant need to cry. She sucked in her breath. "When I was standing on the doorstep of Peter Evans' house…"

His smile fell. "I hate that you did that. I've mentioned it about a hundred times, right?"

She touched his lips. "Let me finish."

"This will be in relation to the question I asked you?"

She nodded. "It will. I told him that he was lonely, that he was doing this because he was so afraid of being alone. In that moment, I understood, not because I was afraid of being alone, but because I wanted to be with you. I would have lived forever missing you."

"Yes, but not committing crimes. Starting over. Eventually finding yourself again. You're so strong and not nearly too much of anything."

Oh the things he said. "Yes, I'll marry you, Elliot Boothe. I'll marry you."

He let out a breath. Had he really been worried? "Thank you, my love. Thank you."

"No, thank you for holding off the void. Thank you for being so strong. Thank you for being my forever."

He kissed her, and she let the heat of it move through her. She'd been cold for so long. But the ghosts were gone except for studying them and there was only a life full of laughter. A comedy, not a tragedy. And the magic that came from loving Elliot.

AFTERWORD

* * *

Thank you so much for reading the Wards and Wands series. If you enjoyed it I have over 80 books published that you might like to check out, spanning most genres in romance. Please visit my facebook group to chat with me and others here: https://www.facebook.com/groups/rebeccasrandomness or my website www.rebeccaroyce.com for more information. Please turn the page for a complete list of my books and to learn more about me.

ABOUT THE AUTHOR

As a teenager, I would hide in my room to read my favorite romance novels when I was supposed to be doing my homework.

I am the mother of three adorable boys and I am fortunate to be married to my best friend. I live in Austin Texas where I am determined to eat all the barbecue in town.

I am in love with science fiction, fantasy, and the paranormal and try to use all of these elements in my writing. I've been told I'm a little bloodthirsty so I hope that when you read my work you'll enjoy the action packed ride that always ends in romance. I love to write series because I love to see characters develop over time and it always makes me happy to see my favorite characters make guest appearances in other books.

In my world anything is possible, anything can happen, and you should suspect that it will.

I'd love to hear from you! Please visit my website at www.rebeccaroyce.com to sign up for my newsletter and learn about my books!

Here's where you can find me online:

Rebecca's Randomness Reading Group https://www.-facebook.com/groups/RebeccasRandomness/

https://www.rebeccaroyce.com

https://www.facebook.com/authorrebeccaroyce/

www.twitter.com/rebeccaroyce

Instagram: rebeccaroyce79

MeWe: RebeccaRoyce
Cheers!!
Rebecca

OTHER BOOKS BY REBECCA ROYCE...

Wings of Artemis

Kidnapped By Her Husbands https://amzn.to/2BQdUxy

Rescued by Their Wife https://amzn.to/2Rr9as4

Crashing Into Destiny https://amzn.to/2VkyXRL

Meeting Them https://amzn.to/2BLPaXm

Reclaiming Their Love https://amzn.to/2GKAw8E

Loving Them https://amzn.to/2BKDmEK

Ship Called Malice https://amzn.to/2BNputj

Saving Them https://amzn.to/2SsrBtH

Dark Demise https://amzn.to/2VidXv3

Light Unfolding https://amzn.to/2GO6Yqr

Still Waters https://amzn.to/2CFePT8

Rising Tides https://amzn.to/2MCdTlM

Lost Star (coming soon)

Pointed Arrow (coming soon)

Last Hope (completed series)

Tradition Be Damned

Past Be Damned

Destiny Be Damned

Compassion Be Damned

Future Be Damned

Dragon Wars (completed series)

Forever

Eternal

Always

Evermore

Endless

Wards and Wands (completed series)

Hexed and Vexed

Curse Reversed

Meow, Baby (novella, co-written with Ripley Proserpina)

Tragic Magic

Safe Haven

Everywhere and Nowhere

Dimension X (coming soon)

More coming soon....

Soul Bound

Prisoner of the Dragons

More coming soon....

Shadow Promised

Strange Days

Weird Nights

Bizarre Years

More coming soon...

The Warrior (completed series)

Initiation

Driven

Subversive

Redemption

Justice

Eye Contact

Embraced

Unlawful (coming soon...)

The Outsiders

Love Beyond Time

Love Beyond Sanity

Love Beyond Loyalty

Love Beyond Sight

Love Beyond Expectations

Love Beyond Oceans

Love Beyond Flames

Love Beyond Lies

Love Beyond Death (coming soon)

Cascade (completed series)

Haunted Redemption

Phoenix Everlasting

Fragility Unearthed

Persuasion Enraptured

Reverse Harem Story (completed series)

Unconventional

Unexpected

Undeniable

Kiss Her Goodbye (completed series)

Hard Truths

Dark Truths

Deadly Truths

Shifter World

Planet Bear

Planet Wolf (coming soon)

The Swamp

Hidden (coming soon)

Stand Alone Titles

Under The Lights

No Quitting Allowed

Mr. Wrong

Bite Marks

Bitten Surrender

The Vampire and The Virgin

Demon Within

Crimson Lust

Call Me Crazy

The Storm (writing with Ripley Proserpina)

Lightning Strikes

Thunder Rolling

The Deluge (coming soon)